Hipbones swayed ever so slightly as she widened her stance. Hands mingled in that silky dark hair that the heat of our situation now curled in wispy ringlets around her face. Finding the filigreed barrette, she unbound her hair, shook her head, and let her true self begin to emerge. She combed her fingers through the cascading hair. My wild Hungarian gypsy appeared as she leveled a gaze into my heart with those blue eyes. Her smile closed, held a long moment, then her tongue, slowly, oh so slowly, wet her lips.

Words

From The River

Deborah J. Collins

Creative Works Publishing
Canton, Ohio

This is a work of fiction. Any similarity to persons living or dead is
purely coincidental.

Printed in the United States of America on acid-free paper

Cover design by Victoria M. Brunk-St. Christopher and Koz
St. Christopher

Library of Congress Cataloging-in-Publication Data

Collins, Deborah J.
  Words from the river / by Deborah J. Collins.
    p. cm.
  ISBN 1-930693-95-8 (pbk. : acid-free paper)
  1. Lesbians--Fiction. 2. Florida--Fiction.
  I. Title.
PS3603.O548 W67 2002
813'.6--dc21

                                        2002000362

DEDICATION

For Linda J. Kolange
   my friend, companion, lover,
   my munchkin.
   Every woman should be so blessed.

Chapter One

A Stop At The A & P

1957
It might come as a big surprise, but a lot of my lesbian history is held in my memory of the space contained by the tongue-and-groove oiled floorboards and the four ceiling fans of the Hastings' A & P with its two red entrance doors. At six years old, I had to walk beside my Mom as she pushed the creaking cart down four and a half narrow aisles. Good Southern ladies (even at six) *do not* stray from their appointed station or stick their hands into the milk box to clutch Gustafson's quarts of milk (not acceptable to cool off just a little from the Florida heat or to get a better peek of Mama and Papa Gus on the label). Mama Gus always reminded me of my Aunt Bird.

Both wore wire rims long before the Beatles made them cool. While my Mom shopped and chatted, greeted both black and white by first name and kept a running mental total of every penny spent, I looked at everyone we passed. Not the kids–the mothers. Those were the days when farm ladies wore only town dresses to market and wouldn't be caught dead without necklaces and earbobs to accessorize them. To me, they were like the beautiful women in the *Modern Screen* magazines my Mom read (unbeknownst to the other ladies of the church Wesleyan Circle). Beautiful women with curled hair, fancy shoes, long legs caressed by nylons and Southern accents that would melt your heart faster than a popsicle in the sun.

I'll admit, I've always been partial to clothing with a shirtwaist design. It did something to those ladies' figures that made you just want to climb on two fifty-pound sacks of scratch feed and jump into their arms for a hug. That last part is true fantasy, of course. Only heathen children would run and jump in the A & P.

I loved Saturdays. I loved the A & P. The Fates, more often than not, would smile on me at the coffee-grinding machine. If it was a moderately slow day, Miss Kate, the grocery cashier, would let me help grind our coffee. The machine-red body with silver hopper and the words, "The Great Atlantic and Pacific Tea Company" printed in bronze letters on the side, was by the cash register. To reach it I had to step up on the wooden crate that held the brown paper bags. Miss Kate would engulf me from behind, reaching strong arms around me to help hold the bag and steady the wobbly crate. That, my friend, was my first step toward the physical bliss of women.

Holding me tightly, but tenderly, Miss Kate–who smelled of freshly ground coffee and a perfume more haunting than anything my Mom owned–operated the green start button. I always prayed the machine would grind *very, very* slowly.

As I clutched the ground and bagged coffee in one hand, Miss K would twirl me around carefully on the crate, bunch me to her for a help down and kiss my cheek as my patent leathers hit the floor. That's when I could get the touch and smell of Niagara starch in her crisp, white blouse and feel a bosom much more endowed than my Mom's. The blouse was always accented with a black scarf-tie and her silver A & P pin (I would tell any therapist today that is when I became obsessed with women in uniform).

Mom would carry the big bags that Miss K packed. Miss K always put the coffee in a small paper bag along with a package of Wrigley's gum. Always, as she handed me the bag, she would wink and say, "Gum is free for my best helper of the week." I'd always smile and wink back as Mom and I walked through the two red doors.

1964
Hastings in 1964 was a bustling Florida farm town. The crops for two years had been exceptional and farmers' wives were sporting new Cadillacs down Main Street to prove it. Sidewalks were crowded. Every store from the Western Auto to Dalton's Cleaners felt the kind hand of progress. Our pastor would have said that God was surely smiling on us all.

I felt God was gracing everyone with his benevolence but me. Maybe it was because I was 13, or maybe it was because of what my Mom warned, "The curse of this family touches you. It will be so very hard if you follow that demon."

Now, I tried taking the warning to be a significant portion of last Sunday's service I had rebelliously refused to attend, but I knew better. My Mom spoke those words as she navigated our '56 blue and white Chevy into the parallel parking spot in front of the A & P. I stared out the passenger window long after she had slammed the door and gracefully sashayed toward the store. Mr. McQuaig, heading for the barbershop next door, held the red door for her and tipped his hat. He was the kind of man who believed the South would never be too busy to show a touch of gallantry.

That Saturday marked a gulf that would widen the heart space between my Mom and me–though no one would ever see it.

That was the day I wore my overalls into the A & P. Today the act would be so commonplace, so unnoticed, but to my Mom, who *always* dressed for shopping, who *always* had an extra embroidered hanky in her purse, who wore my Dad's worn-out dungarees *only* to shrimp from their boat in the late-night hours of August, this was the *ultimate* social sin to be committed. If I wanted all our neighbors to think that I was uncivilized white trash hell-bent on a wild life of nonconformity, drinking, carousing, and total deprivation, all I had to do was open that car door and walk eight steps into the A & P.

After a hard swallow, with sweat pouring down my shirt collar, I took those eight steps and turned the brass doorknob. The red door creaked open, and the bell over the doorframe jingled the death knell.

I calmly surveyed the weekly specials on the overhead chalkboard. Ten pairs of eyes stared at me. As there was a collective intake of air from almost everyone in the room, the Baptist minister's wife stared at me and dropped half a dozen medium eggs onto the wooden floor.

The exception to the collective intake was my Mom. She was at the back of the store humming a Frank Sinatra tune in time with the radio that sat on the top corner of the detergent shelves.

I couldn't imagine what havoc I had cast to my future fortune with those overalls . . . but far in time, I would learn.

We took another breath and continued our appointed tasks. Mine was at the back of the store to push the buggy for Mom.

We shopped. Mom chatted, directed me to get what she needed from the top shelves and discussed if we really wanted to shell Crowder peas for Sunday dinner. Not a word or sign–not even a raised eyebrow– was given concerning the controversial clothing.

That thirty minutes of shopping was capped by Mrs. Ellis and her daughter, Mamie Jo, entering the store. She wore, of course, a neatly-ironed blouse with a Peter Pan collar, a new J. C. Penney skirt, bobby socks, and penny loafers. My Mom looked at Mrs. Ellis' daughter and back at me. Enough said.

We went to the cash-out and I started to unload the items. First, frozen, perishables and bread, to be bagged separately, then canned, boxed, glass, cleaners, and pet food. My Mom was Prussian with the unloading rules. I was making good headway with the boxed when

Mom said, "We forgot dog food. Go out back, please.
Fifty pounds should do. Red bag. Dog face on the front."
I knew it was a blue bag with running hounds that was
needed. I nodded and walked back down the center aisle.
    The A & P had a back room for extra stock and a
closed-in back porch that doubled as the grain and pet
food area. "Canned" was dispensed from cut-open cases
and "bagged" from pallets. The center of the pet food
room had double screen doors that opened onto a roofless
loading dock adjacent to the alley behind the block of
downtown stores (I doubt much left through those double
screen doors unpaid for). Mostly, the alley was used by
kids on bikes as a shortcut from the Five & Dime at one
end of town to the Standard Oil station at the other.
    As I approached the opened doors, I saw Mr. D.
L. Bennett's pickup truck parked behind the grocery. His
son, Dennis, sat illegally in the driver's seat making time
with Mamie Jo, standing on the loading dock. While she
talked, she smiled and flashed sky-blue eyes at him.
    "C'mon, Mamie Jo. I'll drive you back to the farm.
We'll follow your mother when she pulls off Main Street
by Stanton's."
    "How will Mother know where I am?"
    "I'll be glad to tell her," I said as I walked a step
behind M.J. and stared down Dennis over her shoulder.
An easy task. I was a head-and-a-half taller than M.J.
and a head taller than Dennis.
    Dennis returned my glare over M.J.'s shoulder and
let out a whoop of surprise. "Well Debbie–no–I mean
farmer Collins, that would be real kind. Real kind,
indeed." Those words were said with what sounded like
the best laugh Dennis Bennett had had all week.

M.J. turned, full back to Dennis and looked at me up and down. "Thanks, Diane, I owe you," she whispered. Dennis and I never had hit it off. Your daddy having more money than God did not mean you could diagram sentences in English class. He hated smart girls. "All right, then! Hop down here and let's go!" he demanded as he leaned over and pushed open the passenger door.

Dennis would never have Mr. McQuaig's gallantry.

M.J. protested, "There's mud in the ruts and I have on my good shoes."

I believe she was looking for a way out of what her flirting had accomplished.

"Aw, damn! Just get in the truck!"

Dennis was not about to get his Dingo boots dirty.

M.J. looked shyly back at me for help.

I melted. Her eyes were so very, very blue. What's a girl in overalls to do? I stepped down the two steps of the loading dock and turned to face her. "Just hop down to me, and I'll see you get to Mr. Bennett's truck safely."

I had no idea how to do that, but with more faith than me, M.J. bunched up her skirt and leapt just as she would toward our favorite swimming hole at Pellicer Creek. As the wind and sun caught her blonde hair and set it wild and sparkling, I caught Mamie Jo Ellis in my arms.

We howled with laughter–she, at my ability to make a successful catch, and I, at her blue eyes that never left mine as I walked about three yards to the truck and placed her, with dry shoes, in the seat beside Dennis. I closed the door and kept my eyes on M.J.

Dennis revved the truck . . . eager to go.

"Wait! Just wait!" insisted M.J.

My hands were gripping the top of the rolled down window as she bent down to her shoe and removed a shiny '64 penny. She straightened up, unglued my hand from the window and folded the penny into it with both her hands cupping mine. As she did so, those lovely, deep-river blue eyes never left my gaze.

"Good enough wages for a fisherman–not even a real farmer," sneered Dennis as he swigged on a Mountain Dew.

"No wages at all, Dennis," she said loudly to him. "Simply a token of my affection," she whispered to me.

Dennis never heard the last part over the gunning of his daddy's V-8 engine.

I put the penny in my pocket as the pickup jostled down the alley to make a left toward Main.

Foregoing the flat dolly, I grabbed the sack of dog food and, chucking it onto my shoulder, headed toward the store's center aisle. Mrs. Ellis was putting three cans of Del Monte sliced beets in her buggy when she caught sight of my approach.

"Mrs. Ellis, ma'am, Mamie Jo went with Dennis to meet you at Stanton's. He was loading at the back dock and kindly asked her. She hoped you wouldn't be mad. Nice young man, that Dennis."

"Thank you, dear," she coldly acknowledged. "I'll be done here in five minutes."

Mrs. Ellis had waited for the beginnings of a romance between those two forever. Only the Ellises, she reasoned, would have money and land enough to marry into the Bennetts. She was tending to think that God did answer prayers.

"Mrs. Collins paid already. Take it to the car and meet her at McElveens'," ordered the checker without missing a beat on the black and white price keys.

"Yes, ma'am."

Yes, ma'am, indeed! I thought and smiled as I loaded the fifty pounds into the backseat, wiped my hands on my handkerchief and stuffed it into my pocket, feeling the penny. Walking down the block, I said a silent prayer for having thrown my Dad's cast nets a million times. I probably had more body strength than Dennis Bennett could ever dream of.

Mr. McQuaig, long finished with the barber, sitting with his friends for a Saturday ritual of gossip and camaraderie, tipped his hat as I walked by the open barbershop door.

"Miss Collins, a graceful completion of your task. You carried that fifty pounds with strength and style. Young ladies don't usually work summers, but if you should ever need to, let me know."

"Thanks, Mr. McQuaig. With permission, I just might take you up on it, sir. I want to go to college," I replied, smiling at Mr. McQ and seeing a pair of overalls just like mine.

"They're real functional–practically last forever," he chuckled.

I laughed and walked on. Mr. McQ knew real capability when he saw it (Several years later I took him up on the job offer. The best employer I ever had).

I met Mom at McElveens' and carried back the three pounds of 6-D nails my Dad wanted.

Mamie Jo Ellis wore penny loafers with only one penny the rest of the school term. Dennis Bennett never learned the correct principles of sentence diagramming.

Years later, at their wedding reception, M.J. inquired about the "token of affection." I told her I had it–and probably always would.

"It's just . . . well . . . my folks expect us to be together," she said as I held her hands in a congratulatory shake.

"Of course," I replied, oblivious to everything but those sky-blue eyes, knowing others could hear. "You will do it with strength and style."

"To this day," she confessed, "Dennis refuses to get his Dingos in the mud."

"Indeed, then what possibilities missed," I whispered as I kissed her cheek, not in wedding celebration but in good-bye.

1973

Christmas break of 1973, I came home from college with a lot of baggage–most of which didn't have to be carried into our house like the two duffels my Dad took from me and demanded that he see to. That was my Dad's warmest type of welcome–his seeing to something. Hugs and kisses from him would happen only after Mom got her turn first at the door.

My Mother held the door as Dad proceeded up the steps and into the house. After so many trips home, he knew exactly where Mom would expect the duffels to be placed in my bedroom.

With Dad busy inside, she let the screen door go and opened her arms to me. My Mother was tall, thin and worked to death by the time I arrived in our family. Her frail arms wrapped around my neck belied her true strength. She hugged me as if this was the last time we might embrace. Secretly, in my heart, I feared that it might be so.

"Child, you are so thin, and your top shirt is missing a button! I'll sew it on right after supper." All those words rushed out of her too fast, as tears ran down her cheeks.

"Mom, this is Amelia–Amelia Wakefield." I turned and nodded to the young woman who gazed at my Mother and me and surveyed our modest home with intense inspection. She had not taken one step from the side of the third-hand VW, after closing the door.

"Amelia, my dear Miss Wakefield, come. We're so please and honored to have you visit. Diane has told us so much."

With that, my Mother left the porch and guided her back to where I stood. My Mom never took a person's hesitation as a sign of discomfort. She considered it their being only unfamiliar with their surroundings.

As she walked with Amy, Mom spoke, "I'll show you around, and you two can talk to me while I finish up supper."

My Dad came out, finished with his chore and hugged me and planted a big kiss on my cheek. Amy laughed, then caught herself.

"It's fine, Miss Wakefield, enjoy the joke. I've had to stand on tiptoes to hug her since she was twelve." He released me with a pinch to my cheek and demonstrated the same greeting to Amy. He didn't have to tiptoe. She was exactly my Dad's height.

"It's just that I'm wearing these boots–thick soles," I reasoned, as I shooed everyone inside.

"Diane, I'll get Miss Amelia settled, and you help Dudley with the nets."

"It's Amy, Mrs. Cole, just Amy."

I knew that they would get along. Heading toward the back door, I announced to no one in particular, "I'm out back." Mom's and Amy's low chatter and laughter from the kitchen told me I'd not be missed for a few minutes. My Mom would have Amy's life story before the biscuits were out of the oven.

I pressed my hand to the wooden brace in the middle of the screen door and stepped down onto the porch. I closed my eyes, held my breath, then slowly opened them and breathed as my boot felt the homemade rag rug that lay beneath it.

Would the scene I was about to see be magical this time? Would it be just as it had been since I was a toddler who stood and peered under the screen door brace, fingertips laced through the wide wire screen door secured by the hook and eye I couldn't reach?

Letting the screen door go, I gazed beyond me. It was so spellbinding, so beautiful. Just as wild and pristine, just as dangerous and seductive as I remembered. It was the same scene I'd conjured up a thousand times when closed in by big city buildings, jostled on subways or caught in a factory filled with smoke and fumes.

Before me lay four and a half miles of open water. Whitecaps skimmed the bluest of blues, pushed shoreward by a gentle northeast wind. Stately cypress and 200 year-old oaks lie between me and my Dad on the dock. Seagulls flew mid-channel as herons and egrets hugged the edge . . . slowly, purposefully hunting, always hunting. Ospreys perched on cypress knees. Soon-to-be storm clouds formed beyond the tops of the far shore trees. The sun, setting early in winter, painted the sky with bands of lavender, gray, rose-pink, and crystal blue that stretched from the river's bend at Federal Point to the channel light at Picolata eighteen miles away. My view was engulfed in sounds–screeching gulls, warning birds, the clanging of distant bell buoys, lapping waves hitting the shore and dock, and the ever-present wind, which tonight, was mournful and desolate.

I was home. Drinking it all in, I marveled at its beauty once again. Happily, asking no more, I would have lingered on the back porch for the rest of my visit.

"Kid," my Dad yelled, "come help an old man who wants to finish up before the wind picks up and Mom's biscuits are cold."

"Yes, siree! Just let me take my good shirt off," I replied, grabbing a work jacket from the nail on the porch wall. Gone so many years and he still kept my jacket there. As I swung my arms into it, I saw that it obviously had found its way into every weekly wash. It was beginning to fade and wear thin. Crisp folds marked the sleeves. My Mom ironed everything.

I headed for the dock, hands in jean pockets, with the wind flipping the open jacket tails. This winter was unusual, even for Florida. It was a December in the '80s. "A true paradise," I whispered midway to the dock and lingered with the view. As the sun set in earnest, you could feel the rush of night air in the river's breeze.

Dad and I secured the skiff, straightened nets, and stacked trout lines that were folded into Pepsi Cola crates ready for the next baiting. We worked in silence–as a team. I believe that Dad was proud that I remembered so much.

Walking back toward the house, we could see Amy setting the dining room table as my Mother brought bowls from the kitchen.

I put my arm around Dad's shoulder. "Mom's cooked way too much, but it will be great. I can't wait."

"It's her joy, you know. You here with Miss Amelia," he said, never taking his eyes off the house.

Dinner that night was rowdy and a culinary delight. True home cooking mixed with four people talking at once, laughing at tales of escapade of the country and campus, a viewing of all my baby pictures by Amy and my Dad recounting the story of how his almost loss of life destined he'd meet his wife. Over the years, Dad had worked that recounting into a true art form.

I washed the dishes while Amy dried and stacked. Sitting at the table while we worked, my Mom and Dad talked and talked–more talking from them than I'd ever heard before.

The phone rang at 9:30, as we still sat around the table with coffee and the few leftover biscuits. A ring after 9:00 meant trouble.

My Mom got the phone and returned from the front room stern and serious. "Trouble at Hudson. Matthew's in the emergency room. Dad and I need to watch the kids so Helen can be with him."

My Dad was already pulling the car keys off their place by the kitchen door. "Don't forget a sweater, Gracieanne," he reminded as he went to pull the car to the front of the house.

"You never get home–and now this."

"Don't worry. I've got two weeks. Amy and I'll

hold down the house. Call tomorrow–early. We'll come and help with the kids if need be. Take our prayers."

Having family at the paper mill meant that you could always expect injury or worse. Our family had had more than its share. Mom got her purse and sweater, stopping just long enough to change her shoes and was out the door before my Dad made the front drive.

"Your parents are perfect."

"Perfect for the country, you mean."

"No, Miss Worried-I-wouldn't-like-the-woods Collins. Perfect for you," Amy sternly reprimanded as she put the coffee cups and spoons in the dishpan.

I sat at the table, knowing that one more city girl would probably hightail it on the bus back to civilization come morning.

"Why do you think so?" I questioned, knowing I had enough in my pocket for the bus ticket.

"They're perfect for you because they love you totally–and they just adore me," she said so matter-of-factly, and smiled-one of her wicked come-hither ones.

With that I took her hand and led her to the glider on the porch.

"I thought I'd get to see your river."

"Not tonight . . . way too dark and rain's coming. Besides, it's not my river. It's *the* river," I said as we straightened the cushions. I sat at one end, legs in the seat and nestled Amy in the same position in front of me. She wrapped her hands around one knee and settled into my chest. Raindrops hit the tin roof.

"Right, again, professor. That is uncanny. Could a city girl learn it?"

"Sure. No problem. First lesson tomorrow."

We talked as the rain grew and subsided. The moon meandered between gray clouds, then established its hold on the night.

We spent that night under handmade quilts in one of the twin beds in my room. Time lost in love. Sleep found me with Amy in my arms and brought dreams that said that maybe all was okay. The phone brought the reality of morning.

I ran, only quilted, to get it. "Sure, no problem, Mom. Glad everybody is okay. We'll make supper. Yes, I remember how to cook. See you 'bout 6:00. Love to Dad. Bye."

"Is everything all right?" Amy questioned as she appeared in the bedroom door similarly styled.

"Fine. Just stitches for Matthew, no broken bones. Mom and Dad are staying to tidy the house and get lunch for the kids. Give Helen a little rest. We'll fix supper, okay?"

"Sure."

We dressed, made the bed and started coffee. I urged Amy to get the milk quickly and not settle in the kitchen chairs.

"I'm tired! Just a little rest, right here, okay?"

"No, we're going to the river. Hurry up! Time's important," I demanded, cajoled and pleaded. "C'mon, sweetheart, you've got to see." With that I took her hand, and we walked to the end of the dock. I sat on an upturned wooden crate and situated Amy between my knees on the dock's edge. "Now listen, and be real still," I whispered as we moved only to sip our coffee.

"Damn, Di, what time is it?" she softly questioned.

Turning my wrist to check my watch, I replied,

"6:52 a.m."

"I'm really ti—,"she broke mid-sentence as she watched the still water that lay in front of us ripple, swell and slowly churn. A small thud sent movement throughout the dock.

"I'm out of here–now! That's no fish. Quick, let me up!"

I held her shoulder gently to beseech her to stay. "They're manatees, Miss Live-in-the-city-far-from-the-river Wakefield. Six to eight of them. They're the river's grace incarnate."

"That last sentence should be a poem title," she half-laughed but kept her eyes on the water, fascinated at what unfolded.

"Any minute now, and don't forget to watch the birds."

As if I held my Dad's psychic link to this water, at that moment, as predicted, the manatees surfaced and circled. Smiling, whiskered faces surrounded two young calves. They spotted us, and the circle edged around the dock end.

Amy grabbed my wrist but still kept looking, "Will they break the dock down? They're *very* close and *big*. Very big."

"No. They're practically tame. My Dad feeds them," I assured her. "He talks to them and feeds them lettuce leaves and sometimes river hyacinth when he can find it."

"And they like it?"

"Mostly the talk, I truly believe. They come every day in the warm months. The winter's so unusual, I knew they'd be here even now."

"It's the most amazing thing I've ever seen!" She eyed the manatees as they lingered to catch a longer glimpse of the humans.

"There's more," I whispered in her ear, bending close to catch the fragrance of her hair. "Look north." I pointed right, and her eyes followed.

Flocks of egrets left cypress tops, circled wide over the river and flew inland. "They're headed to the farms for bugs."

"How far away?"

"Maybe a mile due east, toward the front porch," I replied.

The herons began their solitary travels for food. They left trees and landed so delicately in the water's edge that not a ripple was made. To our left, flocks of crows noisily competed for the sand bars to have drinks and baths in the shallows. Coots, frightened by the crows, flew for the channel and safety. Their low flight left a rain of spray on the water as their wings and feet touched the surface.

"It's beautiful. I'm so, so glad I didn't miss it. Thanks, Di."

"Finish your coffee. What do you say we get a little rest before going to Hastings for groceries?"

We didn't get rest. We watched the river, and I worked hard to show Amy the river through my eyes. She paid my toils with the softest kisses I've known.

By early afternoon we made Hastings. I drove the two full city blocks for Amy to see it all–two banks, gas station, five and dime, the Western Auto, Stanton's Automotive, hardware, barbershop, city hall, library, the A & P, farmers' co-op, Dalton's, Canaday's, post office,

drugstore and the train depot, which were interspersed
with half storefronts of brokerage and trucking firms. I
named every store and their owners, U-turned at the
depot, and diagonally parked near the A & P.

She sat looking at the storefronts, and the folks
who passed near us walked a little slower past the VW
to get a good look at the stranger in town.

"It's so . . . well . . . unbig, and the buildings . . .
such detail," she exclaimed.

Architecturally, she was right. The Work Progress
Administration had given my town its revamped character.
Every family here had kind words for Mr. Franklin Delano
Roosevelt, whether they were Republican or Democrat.

"Don't you think it's a snapshot from the past?" I
queried. "Maybe part of a time the next generation won't
even care to learn about?"

"I do, and those two ladies, coming down the sidewalk, see those print dresses, patent leather bags and
shoes, *hats*. Are they not just too quaint for words!"

As she spoke, Miss Melvina and Miss Elaine
Canaday, owners of the women's dress shop, approached.
Miss Melvina steadied Miss Elaine with one arm and
waved a hanky toward the car with the other hand.

"Diane Marie Cole, I declare," Miss Elaine
shouted just a tad too loud, "get out of that automobile
so we can get a better look. Is that your sister? No—who's
the young woman with you?"

Everyone within earshot knew Miss Elaine always
liked to have first crack at any Hastings news.

"Time to meet the sisters," I said. We got out and
stepped up to the sidewalk. I gave Miss Melvina and Miss
Elaine their customary kiss on the cheek. They beamed.

"Your mother said you'd be home. You're so busy with school we never expected you'd come to town," Miss Melvina spoke for them both, as they hugged me.

"My friend, ladies. Miss Amelia Wakefield of the Chicago Wakefields. At the river now, for a much too brief visit."

They nodded a greeting and eyed Amy, noticing not only physical appearance but also the cut of slacks and blouse, the materials used and her shoes. I'd expanded on Amy's personal history because I knew they'd like a tangible connection to my friend.

"Why, gracious, grandfather was from Chicago! Came south, though, just after the War." Miss Elaine meant the Civil.

"Better opportunities," added Miss Melvina.

To my surprise, Amy approached each sister and hugged and kissed her on the cheek. Gently she shook their hands, which were frail and showing the ravages of arthritis.

"A pleasure, Miss Elaine, Miss Melvina. May I be so bold as to comment on your lovely perfume?"

They nodded consent and glowed.

"Diane, she is a dear. Bring her by the store when you have time. A new shipment of slacks and some lovely cardigans just came in. Amelia would look stunning accessorized with a scarf to match those beautiful eyes." Miss Elaine's eyes twinkled as she spoke, directing her gaze at Amy, then at me.

"Come, dear. We're late for bridge and these ladies are obviously headed for errands." With those words, Miss Melvina encouraged Miss Elaine down the sidewalk. Amy and I kissed them both good-bye. As they left us, Miss Elaine walked close to Miss Melvina and held her arm for support.

"They are just too, too precious!" Amy exclaimed.

"Characters. True Southern characters straight out of Faulkner," I commented as I held the red door for Amy to step into the A & P. She looked around, eyed the buggies and retrieved one. I took the shopping list from my pocket and handed it to her.

"If you need help, ma'am, just holler. I'm going to stock shelves," said a young girl behind the cash-out as she looked at Amy.

"Let's see . . . milk," read Amy off the list.

"First aisle, right side, third of the way down," I replied as I touched her shoulder and pointed her and the buggy in the proper direction. "I'm going to get something in the back."

I walked the center aisle and took in the store. The overhead fans hummed in the warm weather. Still the chalkboard for specials, still the coffee grinder–moved to a new location-still the smell of Murphy's Oil Soap mixed with the tropical aromas of lemons and oranges and the earthy scents of unwashed bulk potatoes and Vidalia onions. Only the metal garland and twinkling lights strung around the interior perimeter spoke of the season. Two kids at the back of the store counted out change and dropped it slowly in the soda machine.

The right corner of the back of the A & P was Mr. Pearson's butcher shop. A 10' x 8' rectangle formed by two refrigerator display cases facing outward as an L with an opening at the L's corner for a hinged plank which served as countertop and gate. Behind the hinged side of the counter, a scale, a roll of brown wrapping paper, and a dispenser of wet sticky tape sat on a small table. Mr. Pearson appeared out of the walk-in at the far wall with a shoulder of pork.

"Why, Diane Cole! A big surprise! Let me store this and help you." He placed the meat in the far display case and turned to face me. "How's the family? Heard about Hudson? Everyone okay?" he asked as he wiped his hands on a white towel tucked into his apron waist.

"Everyone's fine, sir. Matthew had stitches. I'm doing great. It's good to be home," I said as I eyed the meticulously clean shelved displays of meat through the crystal clear glass . . . pork, bacon, and chicken to the right . . . cheese, beef and fish to the left.

"What'll it be," he questioned. "Everything's fresh."

"I know, Mr. Pearson. It always is."

"Miss Gladys only buys ground round and chicken–some pork. She usually gets four pounds of the round. Want that and anything else?"

Mr. Pearson felt my Mom had sent me–like all those times, all those years before.

"Something Mom wouldn't buy," I pondered. "The steaks. Whatever you think is best. Four, if you please." I felt I could splurge; I wasn't buying any bus ticket. Glancing up from the display cases, I saw Mr. Pearson smiling his approval. He turned to the butcher block in the center of the sawdust-covered square to trim and wrap the order.

From the back storeroom, Lyle Smith sauntered toward the butcher area, leaned an arm on the display case, faced me, surveyed me up and down, and stared at me with a mean, mean, grin. "Well, Diane, how's life? How's the big city? Never thought you'd come back here," he sneered and took a drink of the Sundrop he was holding.

"It's good to see her, isn't it, Lyle?" Mr. Pearson commented as he continued with the order.

I didn't respond. Lyle Smith was the only person who had ever beaten me up. I wanted no part of him.

He moved to lounge more of his weight on the display case and bring his face barely inches from mine. Speaking now only in a whisper, "Never thought a damned, Commie, feminist, queer bitch would want to come back for more."

I looked into eyes that were so filled with hatred they cut like razors. I gulped. I sweated, but I didn't move a muscle or take my eyes off him. Lyle Smith was trouble . . . big, big trouble. Looking at his 6'3" and 300 pounds, I could only remember that night at the Hawthorn Road House where we'd had our "encounter."

"Lyle Weldon Smith, that's enough!" Mr. Pearson demanded, but did not raise his voice. The wrapped package landed roughly on the counter as he glared at Lyle.

I'm not sure Mr. Pearson had heard that whispered sentence, but he certainly saw the daggers between Lyle and me.

Mr. Pearson stared down Lyle. I stared down Lyle. Lyle in turn stared me down, repeatedly clenching his fist on top of the meat case. No one moved. No one blinked. Lyle gave in first.

In a loud mocking tone, he said, "See you, Cole. Don't stay away so long." He forced a smile as he acknowledged Mr. Pearson and walked down the center aisle.

I finally breathed and watched his retreat. Amy, in

the same aisle, was putting cornmeal into the buggy and reading the list. Lyle Smith touched his baseball cap in greeting to her as he walked by. She smiled, said hello, then waved to me as she continued shopping.

"Sorry, Diane, real sorry," Mr. Pearson spoke very slowly and very low. "That Smith boy's been trouble since day one."

"It's okay. Our feud," I tried to say jokingly, "goes way back." I took the package from the counter. "Thanks, for everything."

Mr. Pearson nodded then moved toward me in pretense of wiping the counter. I saw a man with sad eyes. "Robert . . . you remember my son?"

"Sure do. Graduated a year above me."

"Well, he . . . uh . . . lives in California now, you see. Won't come home."

I looked at the man in amazement as he continued. "I tell folks it's his work, but he told me before he left it's because of people like Lyle Smith. You know, Robert also told me about your and his ruckus with Lyle at Hawthorne Road. I promised I'd never say a word, but," he spoke with a crackling voice, "you shouldn't have to leave your home and neither should Robert. It's just damn not right. Robert's a fine young man." He held back tears and smiled weakly.

"No, sir, he shouldn't. Not because of Lyle."

Amy pushed the buggy up and caught me gently with its front. "Di, this store is great! Fresh everything and foot tubs–I've never seen foot tubs in a grocery store," she laughed and maneuvered the buggy beside me. "I got some stuff definitely not on the list."

Mr. Pearson's demeanor returned to that of a

smiling store clerk.

"Mr. Pearson, may I introduce Amy Wakefield, my friend and shopping companion."

"A pleasure, Miss Wakefield." Mr. Pearson wiped his hands and reached across the counter in greeting.

"All mine, Mr. Pearson. You have a wonderful store. The gentleman on aisle two, who was kind enough to help me find the celery seed, said you managed this wonderful establishment."

In half an hour, Amy talked as if she was one of the folks. The South, I saw, fit her like the glove of a Birmingham debutante at her first cotillion.

"See you both next time you're in town," Mr. Pearson cheerily said as I turned the buggy toward the cash-out.

"You sure will. Give my regards to Robert. Tell him to have a great adventure in California. Tell him I'm fine and coming home soon."

As we stood in line, I decided that my life would not be lived in two distinct worlds anymore. Life was way too short, and people like Lyle Smith were everywhere. Amy, fascinated with the oldest cash register she'd ever seen, chatted with the cashier as I unpacked–in the order I learned from my Mom. I left the store with one last wave to Mr. Pearson.

We stored the groceries in the VW, and I asked Amy if she wanted ice cream–teasing that it was the best this side of Palatka. It was, in truth, the only this side of Palatka.

As we turned toward the street, Amy spied a small box tied with string and a small enveloped card tucked securely beneath the string's knot in her car seat.

Picking it up, she exclaimed, "It's for Miss Amelia Wakefield. Is this a joke of yours or what?"

"Don't have a clue, but being here such a short time you must already have an admirer," I replied, as curious as she as to what the box held.

Amy undid the box as fast as a six-year-old with Christmas gifts. Inside, wrapped in the fanciest, sheerest paper with a gold Canaday paper sticker to secure it, were two tiny cut-glass bottles of very expensive perfume nestled securely in the box upon a lady's "carrying" hankie. The delicate handkerchief of fine Irish linen was bordered by pulled threadwork while intricately embroidered violets marked each corner.

"It's the most lovely gift. Those ladies are too sweet," Amy said as she held the box close to her face to take in the scents.

"I'll hold the box. Read the card," I demanded as eagerly as another young child.

She unsealed the envelope. The card read:

Dear Miss Amelia,
Our perfume as a remembrance of our lovely meeting.
Hope you can find them in Chicago.
D.C. will know about the hanky. She's the
Medieval historian.

Sincerely,
E.C. and Melvina

Amy looked puzzled and very surprised. I smiled to myself, knowing that it's true–we're everywhere.

"What about this dainty hanky? Something I don't

know? Isn't this just too, too sweet? The perfume bottles are priceless in workmanship," she observed, taking the box from my hands. "C'mon, what's with the hanky?"

"Well, if you must know," I dragged out the sentence to see her fidget just a little more. She was beautiful in her expectation. "Medieval courtly types–the women, that is–gave them to men who held their affection. Miss Elaine and Miss Melvina surely took a shine to you–what a gift. So romantic. Who's getting the symbol of your undying affection come Black Plague or Crusade?" I asked sweetly.

"Why, of course, you, Miss Diane." With that she hugged me, gave me a kiss on the cheek and patted the handkerchief into my pocket.

As we hugged, I glanced over the top of the VW and through the passing cars to see Lyle Smith across the street slouched on the bench in front of the Western Auto.

"C'mon," I said, "there's ice cream waiting for the ride to the river."

1986

On a Friday at the end of October, I was deep in concentration over which cabbage to buy, when Valerie McKenzie silently approached me from behind, put a well-manicured hand on each of my shoulders, and whispered, oh, so sexily in my ear, "Why buy it, sweetheart, when you can get it for free?"

I laughed, because Valerie McKenzie's daddy grew cabbages, and turned around until she stood beside me. We both hefted a cabbage and looked at the produce display. You know, just a couple of shopping wives finding the best bargain.

"Just where have you been, Diane?" she demanded to know in mock sternness. While she tenderly rubbed the cabbage with the first two fingers of her right hand, she glanced my way with a wicked, wicked smile, waiting for a reply.

"Around. Busy. Working. Putting my life in order," I responded, still standing with bowed head toward the cabbages. There was no need to expand with details. Valerie McKenzie knew me better than anyone else.

"What you need is diversion–no, an adventure, my friend."

With that statement, she made me put the cabbage down, put her arm around my shoulder and shooed me out of the A & P. Everyone said hi to us on the way out. Valerie dropped enough "Darlings" and "Sweethearts" to have planted a molasses field. I only acknowledged those folks with a nod. Holding back tears left no energy for conversation. I held the red door as she made a very slow exit. There was one last wink and coy, Scarlet O'Hara wave to the bag boy.

She guided me to the passenger side of her convertible, parked two storefronts down. As she sauntered around the back of the car, two members of the Hastings Volunteer Fire Department stuck their heads out of the barbershop door for a friendly wave to Valerie. She smiled, waved and donned sunglasses. Turning on the radio, she hit reverse, left the space, then squealed her tires down Main Street. I grabbed the armrest and pushed both feet into the floorboard. Valerie did fifty in a twenty-five to the only stoplight in town and hung a right.

Over the radio she yelled, "We need supper. Colonel S okay?"

I nodded in agreement, fished in my shirt pocket for sunglasses and settled back for the ride. Colonel S was twenty miles away in the next town. To myself I thought, "She's still hell on wheels."

That's one word I always associated with Valerie–hell. Hell as in break the rules, push the limit and the law. Try anything once, never leave till you've had a good time, and always be the center of the universe–wherever you are, whatever it takes.

We took those twenty miles in record time. As she drove in true NASCAR style and focus, I thought about my first meeting with Valerie Adelle McKenzie.

We were eight years old. She was a newcomer to the Baptist Church Sunday School class. On the second Sunday she attended, she told the teacher her daddy said we were all going to hell in a handbasket. It seems Mr. McK was Catholic and, with no Catholic church in town, he'd relented to his wife's Protestant demands for his daughter's Christian education. After that Sunday, I didn't see Valerie until she arrived next term in my school class.

Inseparable, that's what we were. We even kept in touch through the summers. I would beg my Mom to drive to their farm so we could play. There were sleepovers and birthday parties. School dances and football games when we got older. Through my friendship with Valerie, I learned that opposites do attract.

In fifth grade, as we sat behind Mr. McK's barn sharing one of his illegal Cuban cigars, Valerie and I pledged to be not best friends ("So trite," she said), but confidantes ("More truly bohemian," I said). The pledge held through her abortion in high school, two ex-husbands who left her with the convertible and 1,000 acres of prime timberland in the next county, and her fears of never finding true love. It held through my college years, broken relationships, four jobs, and the realization that finding true love may not have a happy ending.

That pledge held today as she slowed through Palatka and headed for the Colonel S. As we waited to pick up the order at the drive-through, she patted my hand and softly said, "You've cried enough, damn it. No more tears. Not for her. Not for yourself. You're way too romantic. You should've lived in the 19th century."

After placing the order in my lap and paying the window clerk with correct change and two "Sweethearts" in one sentence, we traced our way back toward Hastings but took the cut-off to Cracker Swamp Road. The McKenzie farm was four miles on the left. We made very good time.

"We're eating on the porch," she declared as she pulled the car to the barn side of the gravel drive. Valerie headed toward the house on the left of the drive. "I've just got to have wine. Set the table, please."

I carried the bag dutifully to the low rough-plank table that sat on the porch's front edge. It was strategically placed a good foot from the full breadth of a real push of the porch swing. Pulling napkins, boxes, plastic containers and disposable ware from the bag and arranging them artfully (I positioned the picture of Colonel S on the chicken box toward the swing), I announced, "Dinner, Madame. No formal attire required."

"Thanks, m'dear," she drawled in politeness as she handed me a wine glass and settled herself on the porch's edge nearest her side of the table.

We'd eaten breakfast, dinner, and supper on that

porch edge more times than I could remember. Always in the same "formal" ritual–legs dangling off the porch with a napkin in our laps. Valerie McK taught me that there must be style in everything you do.

We munched and talked our way through dinner, only stopping for V to refill the glasses and retrieve more napkins from the kitchen.

"Where're your folks?" I asked, stuffing the dinner remains into the paper bag.

"Hollister, m'dear. Won't be back for a day or two. Daddy's gone to the hunting camp. Mama's visiting third cousins."

"Drop the m'dears. They do not have any effect on me."

"Can't help it, Cole. It's me, you know."

I did know. Valerie was the flamboyant Bette Midler type of Hastings. Style and sweet words could get her most anything she wanted from the citizens of our town and the surrounding vicinity. V McK knew all the tricks. She was, I often thought, way too large for this small place.

"I'll do cleanup," I said as I headed toward the trash in the McKenzie kitchen. "Let's sit on the swing."

Stepping into the kitchen was stepping into the happiest times of my past. The enamel sink, oversized table with benches and chairs, and the Admiral refrigerator were all the same. Only the arrival of an electric can opener broke the spell created by the printed wallpaper and the bread bowl placed on the far corner counter. When I returned to the porch, Valerie patted for me to take my usual spot on the swing.

"There, now. Time to relax," she said as she

combed her fingers through frosted hair and gazed over the front yard toward Cracker Swamp Road. She pushed the swing ever so slightly with her bare toe, and we rocked a slow rhythm in time to the crickets in the yard. Night was just coming on, and a full moon in front of us peeked over the pines beyond the road.

I did the next push with a bare foot, casually laying my left arm on the back of the swing. The other I rested on the swing arm and felt the tension of the moving chain through my fingers on the wood. Another of our rituals–only push the swing with bare feet. Mrs. McK said it was a good idea because it kept a lot of dirt off the porch. Valerie preferred the reasoning that it kept us in tune with our surroundings. Our shoes nestled in the spots we had just left at the edge of the porch.

We sat in silence for a time. Owls spoke. An armadillo slid silently through the shadows between the oak trees. A breeze, ever so soft, with just a hint of fall, swayed the moss on the oaks in the moonlight. At that moment, for the first time in a while, I thought life was good.

"We'll have that adventure tomorrow, Di. I promise, we'll drive to Orlando. Pick up a woman for you and a man for me. C'mon. What d'ya say . . . deal?" Those words came out of her as seductively as the moonlight flowed through the trees. Val McK was never at a loss for effect.

"We'll see," I responded, rubbing my neck and facing her. "You know I'm busy, and I know it's just talk. Have we *ever* done such a thing in say, oh, the last twenty years?"

"Nope, but it's time. We could make it a woman

for me and a man for you. Now, that would be some damn different fireworks than we've ever tried!" Her eyes sparkled in the moonlight as she giggled the proposal.

"We'll see, Miss Valerie Adelle McKenzie." My addressing her full name always signaled that whatever the case was, it was closed. "It's your turn to push."

V. McK charmed me for a good part of the evening, alternately pushing the swing and singing snippets of show tunes. What she forgot in lyric she more than made up for in presentation. Her repertoire had grown from only *The Music Man* in elementary school to include a myriad of songs. Not just the new ones but also those of Mr. Cole Porter–my particular favorites.

That woman never failed to make me happy. She once told me she only sang for me, but I somewhat suspected that many beaus had had such entertainment on the front porch swing. It didn't matter, though. Not really. Tonight she did sing only for me.

While she caught her breath, I talked about everything in general–who I'd seen that we knew and snippets of gossip she'd missed while in the Bahamas, waiting for her last divorce to come through.

She began her singing again, but stopped mid-sentence while doing a *Damn Yankees* number.

"How's your heart, really, Di? I was so sorry that I was so far away when you called. I was real glad Mama gave you the number."

"My heart is, well, broken," I whispered, "but I'll survive. I always do, you know. It's just . . . well, she was the one, Val. My heart's mate. She was planning on moving here and hell to the consequences. We wanted a relationship–a very permanent one. It's been hard as sin.

No one to talk to. Only you know about her and understand. No tears, though, I promise."

With those words, tears came in spite of me.
Valerie leaned over and softly pressed her palms to the
sides of my face, removing my tears with gentle wipes
of her thumbs. The same manner a mother would soothe
a child.

"Always the stoic with a romantic heart," she said
as she hugged me, took the extra dinner napkin from my
shirt pocket and handed it to me. "Do you think we'll get
life right in the next thirty-five years?"

"Not me. I'm not trying anymore."

"Hell's bells, Diane Cole. Get off this swing and
let's do something–something unusual. It's Friday night.
Time to gallivant!"

V. McK always knew how to change the mood of
a room when it got too depressing.

"There's not too much unusual to do eighteen miles
from the nearest stoplight at 11:00 p.m. on a Friday night,"
I smiled and calmly reasoned. We had a running joke
about living in a social and intellectual wasteland.

"C'mon, darling," she said as she grabbed my
hand. "Daddy's got a new tractor in the shed. I know
how you like gadgets."

She led me off the porch at a quick and determined pace. The grass felt great, but when we hit the
gravel drive, we both slowed and picked our path around
the particularly big rocks. We slid open the barn's double
doors and walked in the dark through calm air. No lighting
necessary, having played in this barn a thousand hours
and more. We instinctively knew the path to the second
set of back doors. Even a few small critters scurrying did

not deter us. Sliding the second doors open, we walked out the back of the barn to the open shed where the tractor was parked, glinting moonlight off green John Deere paint that wasn't even dusty.

"Mama vows he's been wiping that tractor down after chores," she informed me, smiling.

"Why not," I replied in appreciation. "It's a real beauty. A true mechanical masterpiece." I didn't have to hunt for adjectives. I love machinery. "A new John Deere complete with cultivator is the capstone of the tractor pyramid."

"Di, you keep talking like that and I'll see you get a job at the Farmer's Supply selling on commission."

We walked around the tractor and took in every little detail. I climbed up to peek at the engine. Val hopped into the cab to check out the radio. Jumping to the ground first, I helped her down.

Valerie spoke as she straightened her blouse and smoothed her slacks. "You know, we're absolutely crazy. Climbing around a tractor at midnight is not what gentile, soon-to-be-over-the-hill Southern belles do."

"It's not," I agreed, "but it sure was fun. Have anything else unusual in mind?" I spoke those words in the spirit of the moment. That's when Valerie Adelle McKenzie hugged my neck and kissed me. Not a fifth-grade practice kiss, but a kiss so sexual, so unexpected, and, oh, so good, I kissed her back.

That's when shock and realization hit me at the same time. I stepped back from her.

That's when the subtle planning and the spontaneity of her efforts hit Valerie. She stepped back from me.

"Well, did you like that, Miss Cole? Was it something

unusual enough?" The unusual was drawn through painfully long syllables.

"Very," I stammered. "Very."

We stood a long, long time in the soft moonlight between the tractor and the barn. I felt as though I was, in reality, standing "between a rock and a hard place." Eyes locked. Intense. No words spoken.

"Hell, you of all people know I'm straight. Too damn straight. I just wanted to–you know–see what the big deal was. What that woman the phone call was about would see in you so different from what I see."

I knew she lied and told the truth at the same time.

"C'mon, my confidante. Daddy's got a stash in this barn of the best moonshine this side of Georgia. What do you say we each remove a pint on the way out?"

Needing a drink, I nodded agreement. She took my arm, and I escorted her back through the barn. We picked two pints off the top row of three stocked shelves, hoping Mr. McK wouldn't miss it. It fell into the category of his illegal Cubans–*Do Not Touch*.

Wrapped in Indian blankets that used to cover us as children when I'd sleep over, we spent the rest of the night on the porch swing.

We talked about hopes dashed and lovers lost, what the future might hold, and why this small town drew us both.

We took our turns and rocked the swing, watched the smiling full moon travel the night sky and sipped its namesake–the smoothest I've ever tasted.

Chapter Two

Sylvia Foster's Mother

I'm supposed to be working tonight, pulling together the outlined notes for a short story, but I am restless and not my usual self. The expectation of bringing notes to fruition usually makes me eager to work, to stay focused–to produce in written word the evidence of my mental labors, but tonight, I've tried with no success. The images of a lifetime ago are haunting me. Images–before the lifestyle of my presumed straightness, before the life-living of my lesbianism–come to mind and demand to find their place on paper. A demanded place as evidence of my threaded journey toward really accepting who and what I am. In many ways it was one of the earliest threads pushed through the eye of the karmic needle that is me.

It is the story of Sylvia Foster's mother.

The summer I was to begin second grade, my Mother and her friends would sit on our front porch in the afternoons to complete a few minutes of handwork and catch a quick break before suppers would be started. At 4:30, when the day was still hot and humid, they would disperse to their kitchens that were more hot and humid than our porch. While they sat for a brief hour, resting from days begun at 5:00 a.m., I'd gather my coloring book and Crayolas and listen, unnoticed, in my corner on the floor to the latest news in my small world and their commentary upon it. This ritual had been going on long before my existence. I was accepted in this grown-up society and clan of these relatives and non-relatives treated like family as long as I kept quiet and did the odd chore, such as getting more ice for their tea or fetching a flyswatter. The flyswatter was usually yesterday's rolled-up newspaper kept tucked beside our two-seated glider.

On one of these summer days, which seemed so like the others, Mother Holtsinger (my godmother's Mother) asked the group if they'd heard about the woman who just moved to Tocoi. She was from out of state–Texas, she thought–a divorcée who had a daughter in the third grade.

The women's continued comments swirled about me as I crayoned a blue lake in my Walt Disney coloring book. My mind raced with possibilities: a girl (there were few my age in the neighborhood), third grade (she'd surely need a friend–me–on the bus around her age), from out of state (someone who'd actually been a part of the Big Outside–that's what I called the rest of the world that was not contained in the territory of our tiny fishing village).

Technically, Tocoi was the Big Outside. It only

drew the distinction, though, of the Outside because I traveled there on the school bus. I colored more quickly and hoped this act of hurriedness would make the time for school begin to move magically closer.

In the weeks that stretched between me and the opening of school, I used every moment to dwell upon the circumstance of a family moving into my realm of existence. It did not happen often. Usually, it was the opposite. Folks moved away when life's struggle failed to produce a farm mortgage or fishing prices fell to an unsustainable level of producing even a meager living for a family. As I grew older, the latter happened with regularity.

Finally, when I thought I would be able to endure it no further, the first day of school arrived. I lay awake the night before, not in anticipation of seeing my city class-mates again, but in anticipation of the bus making a new stop in Tocoi.

My Uncle Fergus drove the school bus. He was kind to me and the other small kids but firm with older farm boys who'd often start a ruckus in the back of the bus on hot afternoons on the long ride home. Uncle Fergus did what few others who drove our bus ever did. He'd stop when time permitted at Molasses Junction and let us use our saved-all-week spending money gleaned from returned pop bottles or extra chores to buy soda or candy at Mr. & Mrs. Pursley's store. I usually feigned serious reading in a library book because we were dirt poor and I'd never ask my folks for extra money.

Many a time he'd ask if I'd split a soda with him since he was only half-thirsty. Way too proud to do so, I'd laugh (which I seldom did) and reply kindly that I was fine. I'd say that he'd better save it because he would be the other half-thirsty by the time we made the River (I was always right. Uncle Fergus never drank the last half of the Coca-Cola until he had turned right at the river).

When Uncle Fergus stopped that big ol' Blue Bird bus for me and my cousins across the road to board, I was antsy with anticipation. All I could manage to say as I pulled myself up by the handrail and climbed the two wide metal steps to the bus floor was, "We stopping extra at Tocoi, Uncle Fergus?"

"Sure are," he said and smiled back as he swung the handle to the door and clanked it shut. He looked in the rearview mirror that stretched across the inside of the bus above the windshield as we found seats. There were plenty, since we were early on. I took one on the right side, mid-center. The bus, grumpy with age, edged forward as Uncle Fergus shifted gears. It was about three and a half miles to the turn-around at the Tocoi fish camp. We re-drove our route to the main road into town, which was one and a half miles before the fish camp.

The morning was already hot, and the bigger boys had lowered the half-windows, which added to the roar the bus made. It was good, though, to feel the wind in your face. The rushing air reminded me of horseback riding or being in my Dad's skiff on the river. All wind-in-your-face things that gave you freedom. I clutched my lunchbox beside me in the seat, sat close to the window and watched the outside move by.

When the bus made Tocoi, I saw a lady and a girl standing on the riverside of the road. I was so happy. I'd be on that side when the bus turned around. The bus groaned, creaked, rattled and slowly made the turn around at the fish camp. We picked up two high school kids who found seats in the back of the bus. They were oblivious to my existence as they passed.

Uncle Fergus edged the bus slowly to a stop where the lady and girl stood. The girl looked like her mother and nothing like the Irish-descended kids already on the bus. Sylvia Foster (who would in time become my bus friend) was tall–very tall–the height of my cousin in fourth grade. She had dark, flashing eyes, shoulder-length curly black hair, and beautiful dark skin that wasn't dark by sunburn but naturally the color of my Mother's coffee when she added just a dash of milk. Her shoes were new and her clothes store-bought. She carried a new McCrory's plaid school satchel. Yes, indeed, here was a person who had experience of the Big Outside. The girl intrigued me, but even more so, the woman who exchanged a few pleasantries in the open doorway with Uncle Fergus before he started moving the bus and clanged the big doors closed.

This woman, who stepped back and gazed at the windows till she found Sylvia in the fourth right seat waving to her, waved back. This woman, who studied the windows further, looked directly at me, smiled and waved again as the bus gained speed. Oh, yes, I was intrigued by this woman who I waved back to by spreading my fingers and placing my left hand on the window glass. I was enamored. Touched in my heart of hearts by her foreign beauty and mysterious smile. Please believe me, I've been enamored since, but in my hidden lesbian-leaning true self, Sylvia Foster's mother holds a foremost place. Not because of a physical revelation (our lives were always separated by the bus window), but because she inspired me to understand what I wanted later in life and how to acknowledge that gut feeling of sudden recognition.

Sylvia Foster and I became bus friends over that school year and played together at recess. She was a grade ahead of me, and by the time the bus route turned into several years, she slowly mingled more and more with the older junior high kids. She was a looker, and the Cochran boys–who also lived in Tocoi and were her age and older–knew it. Sylvia developed natural allure and sophistication into an asset that matched her wit and intelligence. I knew in my heart by the fourth grade why the Cochran boys were smitten so by her.

While infatuated by Sylvia, I remained ever more thoroughly enamored of her mother. Every morning of every stop at her house, of every year, she'd always wave to Sylvia, then search to the middle of the bus and wave to me. Her smile and wave gave me strength to withstand some hard facts that I was learning all too quickly–poor girls from the river were termed "River Rats" and not allowed into the right groups or cliques. My intelligence, which was beginning to single me out among the teachers, could not hide the fact I wore hand-me-downs, scrimped on the use of clean tablet paper, had no extra pencils or never had money for ice cream after school. I was a boon-docks kid who didn't have parentage, social or economic class to possess what my schoolmates took for granted privilege into mainstream society with taken-as-fact college degrees and a June wedding.

Sylvia remained my friend, but as the school years progressed I knew she measured me by the criteria I failed to possess. She blended, melded, swayed and flowed with the capricious rules of the grammar school "right group." I always wanted her to teach me the tricks I never could fully master, even today, how to feel at ease when ill-at-ease is all you know. Instead of asking for help, I silently remained drawn to her by the relativity of circumstance she gave me to her mother.

I've often thought in the years since Sylvia moved away when I was in fifth grade, of the effect she had upon my life and my ability to observe. An even stronger meditation has been her mother. I can picture Mrs. Foster waiting for Sylvia to get on the bus at the end of their meandering drive framed by wild lavender and white azaleas and oaks dripping long lengths of moss. She wears loafers and tailored slacks–something the other women of the neighborhood would dare not do (The liberating '70s were far in our future). A pink turtleneck is covered by a hip-length brown jacket that has a touch of tailored seams and darts to accentuate her small breasts. The jacket sleeves are three-quarter, full, and uncuffed. It is the jacket that is held in my memory as much as the woman who wears it. Two bands of embroidery, hand-breadth in width, grace it. One just below the bust line and one where the patch pockets are placed. The bands are Mexican in theme: donkeys pulling carts, a tall cactus with prickly spines, bold suns and shimmering moons and stars that give way to pyramids and a form crouched in a colorful poncho and sombrero. Those forms and designs were symbols my imagination could speculate about on that long bus ride to school.

Mrs. Foster's clothing was often out of the ordinary (meaning non-utilitarian). It was never like the cotton shirtwaist dresses covered with practical aprons that the other mothers in my neighborhood wore. Her clothing never failed to hold my attention, but it was the woman who sparked a hidden urge in me that I then could not name or even know how to quench. Those physical features so resembling Sylvia's, but deepened and strengthened by age and life, let me know by fourth grade that not only was I attracted to the feminine, but more specifically, to older women. Was it her mystery of maturity that pulled me in? Was it the real, though unflaunted, sexuality she possessed? Was it her control over youth, as Sylvia's mother? Was it that beautiful, soft, true smile that melted my hidden heart and became inspiration for my pre-adolescent poetry? I can't say. I only know I am still enamored of her and enamored of the feelings evoked from me when I catch another, older than myself, woman with my eye of desire. I bless Sylvia Foster's mother for birthing in me the eye of desirous delight in the feminine curve, in the beauty of face, the glint and imagined feel of hair, in the curve of calf, in the imagined feel of caressed breast, and in the form and length of delicately strong hands and fingers. She has inspired me to seek these, have them in reality, and hold them nightly in my dreams of unnamable bliss.

Through those events long ago, yet ever-present in what my heart desires, I am becoming my true self. I have become a steel-forged karmic needle, certain in what I desire but also so caressed by the many threads and types of femininity pulled through my eye that I am awed and inspired by the pattern of design and desire I've discovered I am.

At the supermarket, in a crowded shopping mall, at the theater, at women's music concerts or when joining a new discussion group, I always look, always hope, to see the curve of an older woman's face, the certainty of her eye, the warmth of her smile that will again let me discover Sylvia Foster's mother. The enamoring she has sparked in me has only grown. I am a captive heart of the Feminine in both its strong and reflective sides.

Sometimes, entwined in a lover's arms, safe, secure, no longer haunted by the demons of my childhood, I dream of that beautiful Hispanic woman and the jacket she often wore. In my dream she leads me off a Blue Bird bus with her hand in mine. As we stand amid wild azaleas and moss-draped oaks, she kisses me on the cheek and helps me put on a similar lovely jacket. Then, smiling in approval and appreciation, she takes me in her arms and kisses me full-mouthed. It's a sensuous kiss that holds all the passion of the bold suns and the recognized desire of the shimmering moons and stars our jackets' embroidery portrays.

Chapter Three

Flannel Shirts

Ever since I was a little kid, I've loved flannel shirts. Not those red and black lumberjack types that grace the covers of all the hunting magazines. Not the ones that now, because of Baby Boomer disposable incomes, come in men and women sizes and show that one has more buying power than fashion-hunting sense. No, my friend, I'm talking about those with soft and muted plaids, with colors of palest blues, yellows, and greens—sometimes a rare one with whites and soft salmons and browns–that used to be found ever so often in the J. C. Penney's catalogues and the Sears Wishbooks.

When my brother and I would peruse those dog-eared pages of the men's sections, he would say the shirts were too sissified for "real men." We often had that discussion on the back porch on fall afternoons, out of the way of my Dad finishing up yard work and close enough to the kitchen to smell fresh cherry pie in the oven. Saturdays were my Mom's baking days, and I loved the house on that day–fruity smells mixed with yeasty scents and cinnamon. There was always something cinnamon for next week's lunches.

When I was eight, I decided that "real men" and "real women" did wear flannels, though this was in sharp contrast to the catalogue pictures and my brother's lecturing. Two observations of my own led me to this conclusion:

1). Real men wore them, I knew, because my Dad wore them–even to work. I would never believe from anyone, ever, that he wasn't the realest man in our portion of the county.

2). On cold fall afternoons and during the winter, I'd get home from school, and my Mom would be wearing a worn, but precisely mended, flannel shirt over her house-dress. Usually I would find her in the kitchen where I'd help with finishing up supper–my chore tasks increasing as I grew older. She'd have a bibbed apron with wide tie strings smoothly placed over the shirt. The cuffs would be turned smartly up to accommodate her arm length and the collar of the shirt carefully laid over the apron's neck. Though in chore clothes, my Mom always wore the flannels with what I can only describe as style. The shirts were always as meticulously pressed as her good town clothes.

After supper when the kitchen work was done, she'd sit in our living room to read the paper and watch TV. I do not believe, to this day, she ever watched the television. After reading, she'd knit, crochet, or embroider–always busy hands, always working to make a little pin money or stretch my wardrobe. Today her handiwork would be priceless. Then, it only helped my Dad barely make ends meet.

Bathed and pajamaed, I'd kiss my parents goodnight. Always my Mom first . . . a rule of my Dad who never had many rules for me. Mom would hear me coming and put down her work. Her hug and kiss would enfold me in the feel of the flannels–soft, warm, infused with her scents, and feeling so smooth and comfortable on my skin I wished the hug would go on forever. It was the only time and place of my life I ever felt washed in security.

That's when I started calling them flannels–it was not a piece of cloth, but more like fingers of a wave that would engulf me. Throughout my years of high school, my Mother would remark on my terminology about simple old material in a shirt, but I never stopped. Flannels were different than smooth cotton, chintz, muslin, or silk. Flannels gave a feel to my heart. After high school, my Mother gave up and said my weird phrase was something even a decent education couldn't get out of my head. She'd live with it.

In junior and senior high school I'd wear flannels whenever I could, though I must admit social circumstance and a humid Northeast Florida climate put a dent in the appropriate times. All summer I would pray for an early, wet and long fall to be followed by an extremely cold winter. By mid-spring, I'd resign them to the back of my closet.

At eighteen, I thought my flannels would be lost

to me for good. As far as wearing them was concerned, I made a terrible mistake–the college I chose was two hundred miles *south* of where I lived, and the extremely conservative school presented a handbook which strictly forbade improper attire. There were two pages of women's clothing do's and don'ts, which let me know, in no uncertain terms, into which category the flannels fell.

I packed no flannels to take with me. Late summer found me busy at school with the weather so warm, I slipped into fall without needing my favorite shirts or giving them a second thought. One night in mid-October, taking a break from reading, I tugged open the twelve-paned windows in my room to get a breath of air. Simply by fate, I, a freshman, had been blessed with one of the most beautiful views on campus. My third floor windows overlooked the Hindu Gardens–a complete Hindu temple dismantled by missionaries and sent to the college to be reconstructed, complete with reflecting pool and guarding elephants. On this night, a thin, sliver of moon was mirrored in the pool and palm trees swayed in the night breeze–quiet, serene, mysterious. A scene from E. M. Forster.

As I opened the windows, the coolness–no, chill–of the air took my breath away. The days were so warm still. I breathed in the air and stillness and sat on the windowsill, rubbing my arms that were covered only with a short-sleeved T-shirt. That was the moment I yearned for the flannels. That's when I knew a life transformation was in the haunting stillness of the night. Life was moving ahead on many, many fronts, and the childishness of flannel wishing was to be put away.

A week later, at the campus post office, I picked

up a package addressed in my Mother's flowing cursive hand. Carrying books, package, and hugging my car coat closer, I walked the length of the campus, as trees dropped leaves in the fall evening that brought cold weather in earnest. The wind off Lake Hollingsworth, one hundred fifty yards to my left, whipped small waves and moaned through the trees. It was the first time the lake sounded so much like the river I'd left behind.

The dorm this Friday evening was nearly deserted. Many of the students lived less than fifty miles from campus. Weekends were quiet and almost solitary. I grew to love those long, quiet nights.

Hanging my coat on the door hook, I closed the door and stacked my books on the desk. I quickly opened the package and read my Mom's note tucked inside the first layer of tissue paper:

Dear Di, We are fine and send our love. Your favorite flannel is enclosed and also a new one I feel you will need. The $5.00 is from Aunt Eileen, Uncle J.W., and Mother Holtsinger, for a movie. We know you study much too hard.
Love, Mom & Dad

The crisp five dollar bill was taped to the bottom of the page.

Tears slipped down my face as I continued to open the package. I cried for their unselfish work and encouragement to get me to where I, in reality, had no business to be. My eyes fell on my favorite flannel–crisply ironed and impeccably folded to the confines of the box. Running my hand over the shirt brought more tears. I missed those folks more than I knew and felt a "straight A" average was much too much to ask as payment to remain among the social and academic elite.

I laid the shirt on the bed and the box beside it. With both hands I removed the second flannel. Even new, it held the comfortable feel of wear and the softness of time. A white background was covered with alternating plaids of the palest purple stripes I had ever seen in a shirt. Inch-wide purple plaid alternated with a thin stripe of the same color in both horizontal and vertical directions. The colors were so precisely dyed that it looked like a modern cubist painting.

As I held the shirt by the shoulders in front of me, facing the mirror, I noticed the cuffs and front of the shirt. The spaces between the buttonholes held my Mother's handwork–between each buttonhole, a tiny, embroidered violet flower, alternating in lazy-daisy and French knot and stem stitches. "My Mom," I said aloud, "you knew I'd appreciate the precision of continued alternation no one could actually see." She understood my strange sense of humor.

I folded the new shirt back into the box and tucked it in my bureau drawer. Something so beautiful hidden because women were not to wear men's clothing. That was the first rule in the handbook on the rules of women's campus fashions. My favorite flannel I wore to bed that night and most thereafter of my freshman year.

Several weeks passed, and occasionally I'd think of the flannel shirt imprisoned in the box. A couple of Fridays later, I decided, on the way from supper back to the dorm, that I'd wear my Mom's gift. The Culture Patrol, as we not so endearingly termed the appointed

teachers and housemothers, could not have eyes everywhere on a Friday night.

I showered, changed into blue jeans, allowed on
campus only after class hours, if appropriately tailored
and proportioned (page 42 of the handbook). I put on
the flannel, which fit perfectly and tucked the $5.00 bill
in its breast pocket. Donning my coat and grabbing book
and notepad, I headed for the side hall door downstairs
and the ten-minute walk to the library–my favorite building
on campus.

Not unbuttoning my coat until the second floor
history racks, I found my favorite spot deserted. In fact,
Fridays found the whole floor empty, except for three or
four people on the other side of the room, which held a
lounging area, periodical shelves, and study cubicles.

My favorite spot in the library was on the far end
of the history racks away from general foot traffic. The
end of a double-sided bookshelf faced a floor to ceiling
glass wall with about five feet of carpeted space between
them. That was my spot, sitting cross-legged on the floor
with my back to the bookcase end. No noise, no traffic,
no distractions when the glass wall turned black with the
arrival of night.

For the sake of brevity, and another story in itself,
I must simply say that that is the spot where I was found
by the love of my life this night that I wore my new flannel.
She was an upperclassman, who wore her sexuality like
a passionate badge of courage–no small feat for a lesbian
in this conservative, very traditional place. She introduced
herself, kneeling beside me as I sat on the floor, open
book and notepad balanced, with years of practice, on
my crossed legs. Her closeness sent warm rivers of

desire through me as her hand touched my shoulder and her blue, blue eyes gazed with an intensity that made me want to flee from the demands they exacted from my heart. Demands which I knew, in truth and in my heart–whatever the future held, whatever the consequences–I would only draw closer to and never remove myself from her compelling aura of passion.

After her introduction, which disclosed that she knew much more about me than I did her, she said, "Beautiful shirt. Wherever did you find it?"

"I didn't. My Mother sent it," I stammered, as I lost control of the balanced book. I looked down, unable to meet her gaze, at the papers in disarray. Her eyes, I knew, were searching me with a practiced eye of a woman shopping for what she decidedly knew she wanted.

"You know, it could cause you trouble."

"What do you mean?" I asked, as I, nonchalantly as possible, stacked notepaper into its folder. Something, anything, to keep my concentration from being totally consumed by this beautiful woman. I had to tread carefully. I had heard of women who had been "quietly excused" from the campus for acts so unspeakable–such as kissing on the balcony of Joseph Reynolds Hall–that the handbook dare not even speak the names.

"It's just so queer," she said, matter of factly, in what I thought was much too much a loud voice for the library. As she spoke, still kneeling, hand on my arm, her back to the center of the room, she gave a bewitching smile and winked.

"Don't say that!" I sternly demanded, much too loudly. "There'll be trouble for me . . . big, big trouble. I can't lose the scholarship!" I tumbled out my worries, as well as a warning, in sentences spoken much too fast.

"Not you, Ms. Cole," she calmly spoke as her hand at my elbow urged me to rise. "Your shirt. 'Queer' meaning 'differing from what is usual or ordinary. As in Webster's *NWD of the American Language.*" As she picked my coat off the floor, she continued, "I'm an English major. Take my opinion as completely factual. I love words and know their precise meanings–and their slang considerations."

I stood beside her and met her gaze as she spoke. She offered me my coat in exchange for holding my papers and book. As I put it on, I noticed her leather briefcase that sat near her leg. We stood so close, and as I looked back up from her feet, up her figure to her face, my heart pounding so fiercely, I knew she could feel it, had she placed her hand upon the pocket of my flannel. She calmly stood as I gazed, never making me feel antsy or uncomfortable. I knew she was a woman who appreciated a voyeur.

"Ready to go with me?" she asked.

"With you?"

"Sure," she encouraged as she picked up the briefcase.

"May I carry that for you, Johanna?" I felt emboldened to use her name.

"No, Ms. Cole, you may not," she lectured as we made the first floor landing steps.

My body language told my disappointment as we walked in silence to the library door, which she opened for me.

As we hit the cold night air, she transferred the briefcase to her outside hand and walked so close to me our shadows blended in the commons lights in front of the library. As we reached the night-shrouded walk that ran from the commons to the dorm, I walked in silence as she continued a lively conversation by herself on the symbolism of characters in a recently read novel. When we encountered a deserted stretch of sidewalk, she abruptly stopped, took my arm, and turned me to face her. I could feel her eyes.

"What's the matter? Still upset about the briefcase?"

"Yes, I mean no," I lied.

"You're upset, and never lie to me again. I can read your heart, Ms. Cole," she spoke in the tone of a visiting lecturer.

I stood dumbfounded.

"I've studied you a while. Very difficult, because you are such a scholarly hermit," she whispered the words as she shifted the briefcase in her hands.

"Studied me? For what?" was all I could manage to say. My heart pounded.

"Studied, learned about you, because I find the queer fascinating. Queer meaning that which is singularly out of the ordinary, of course."

The wind picked up. Our faces were struck by infrequent raindrops that fell from a mist that was rapidly enclosing the campus in dense fog. We did not move.

"I wish to have you as my paramour, not my briefcase carrier."

The words were not only startling and totally unexpected, but they were spoken with the softest pleading I'd ever heard. Not a pleading of desperation but a pleading of desire.

The rain began to fall in earnest. We stood in silence.

"Well, is that a "yes" or a "no," Diane. We're getting wet."

"I'm not sure ... yes ... a big yes. I'm still thinking about the part where you knew I lied."

Suddenly realizing that the rain was a torrent, we dashed to the dorm's side alcove and shook our jackets and raked water from our hair.

As she brushed the water from her briefcase, Johanna looked at me and smiled. "Great. I was afraid you didn't know the meaning of the word," she teased as she watched me flip the soggy notepapers, trying to salvage the relatively dry ones.

"Well, it's not one used often in the History Department, but," I reassured her, "I've a friend who's an English major who can help me with the big words that come my way."

"You'll find, Diane, the biggest word I'll use with you is very small–it's *love*."

The woman touched my heart, then, with her absoluteness of knowing me. Years into the relationship, I still marveled at her boldness, her vitality, her singular determination of purpose, and the wisdom far beyond her years. I feared the demons that I saw she was unable to escape.

II. The Shirt Tale Continues

My more than over-romantic leanings led me to believe that Johanna, despite dripping in the freshman dorm alcove, would come with me to my room immediately, so that I could begin my paramour internship. Alas, to the chagrin of my heart, I was wrong. We waited while the rain slowly subsided. She, holding a dripping briefcase in front of her with two hands like a little girl waiting at the school bus stop for the first day of school, stood opposite me and gazed out at the glinting raindrops illuminated by the lamppost light by the alcove entrance. A few people passed us in coming and going–all remarking that we look like drowned rats. Finally, we settled into facing each other, leaning on each side of the open door-way, as the rain slowed even more.

"Would you like to come up, get something dry on, and maybe empty the water out of your shoes?" I tried to add a little humor. The evening had certainly not gone too smoothly.

"No, I'm fine. Stay at this school a while and you'll get used to the unannounced downpours. Guess it's because of being so tropical." As she spoke, Johanna gazed directly at me. Even with the darkness and the distance between us, I could feel those eyes. Those beautiful, deep blue eyes that could become so devilish in a twinkling.

Puddles formed around us on the slate floor. Water from our coats dripped in time to the slowing, almost stopping, raindrops falling from the alcove roof.

She stepped suddenly onto the sidewalk, taking me off guard. "Guess I'll be off. The rain's almost stopped." She turned to the right, toward the Greek houses.

"Wait! Please wait!"

She turned, and laughing, said, "Don't worry, Ms. Cole, I was going to leave a note–a romantic one–for you on your hall card tomorrow, but if you must know, I'll see you on Friday, 7:00 p.m. sharp. I'll come for you." She turned and walked on. Slowly she blended with the night.

My heart was happy . . .so very happy. I watched her until she vanished in the dark. I stood a little longer–imagining her sauntering to the sorority house. Wiping my coat and stamping one last time to remove as much rain as possible, I headed upstairs.

That week of class was the longest and most tedious of my life. Achingly slow. Every hour, every lecture, every incidental of my life moved in torturous time. So anxious, so unwilling to let my mind have time to wander, on Thursday I moved everything in my small dorm room and swept and cleaned. An army barracks never had so much attention. My Friday classes were early, running straight till two o'clock. That left only five hours for me to let my mind wander in only one direction–what I like to call "to womanize."

Friday, 6:30 p.m., found me sitting on my room's windowsill and watching the night engulf the Hindu garden. It had gotten dark early this winter evening, but I sat and gazed through the window long after the day's transition had occurred. Only one small light, a votive candle placed on the temple's altar space, could be seen. It was a picture-perfect night. A full moon was just beginning to gain the sky across Lake Hollingsworth, casting silver beams upon the water and forming shadows through the trees.

Two demanding knocks brought me to my senses. I glanced at my watch–7:02. "She's punctual," I whispered as I headed for the door. My sweating hand opened it slowly.

"Hi," I said. Not a very suave statement to make an impression.

"Hi, yourself. May I come in?" She slowly opened

the door, pushing me, with one hand, gently back into
the room.

"Uh, sure. I'm just a little, you know, nervous," I
stammered as I backed into the room. I backed all the
way to the bed and sat down.

Johanna, surveying the room, took my desk chair,
turned it toward me, and sat down. She positioned
herself casually, almost comfortably in the library chair
by sitting slightly sideways, hanging her left arm over the
edge of the back, and resting her feet on the rungs.

Comfortable, she looked me over. "Come on,
sweetheart, this is your room. Could you possibly look a
little more contented and at ease?"

Wanting her to be at ease, I said, "Sure, let me
just scooch up these pillows and lean back on the bed." I
manipulated the pillows and stretched my legs out on the
bed–after removing my boots, of course. I liked the
position much better. My body eased into the gaze
of Johanna.

"Much, much better." As she surveyed me, I was
afraid that the small space allowed her to hear my heart's
wild beat. "Where the hell is everybody? It's so quiet
around here. Nothing like the sorority house."

"It's the weekend. Most girls go away."

"Very interesting. Seeing you're not the gabbiest
person I ever met–what do you say we just talk. Practice
for you, okay?" She smiled seductively and kept her seat
in the chair.

Talk. That is what we did. I never wanted to learn
so much about anyone. I wanted to know everything: her
favorite peanut butter, her favorite toothpaste, how she
felt about Viet Nam. I drank in her words like the truly

thirsty lover I hoped to be, but I found, to my surprise, with this person of such commanding presence, that I talked as much as she. To talk about myself had always been a burden, and I don't know why. Johanna eased the words from me by truly listening to everything–whether it was about my favorite cat or my philosophical views on reincarnation.

A wailing siren broke our concentration. It was close, too close, turning onto McDonald Avenue that cut the campus.

From her seat, Johanna glanced out the window, following the sound. "It's late," she observed.

"How in the world do you know that?"

"The moon. I'm a follower of the moon. See, it's almost mid-sky." She rose and sat on the windowsill, still gazing at the night sky. "You've a beautiful view from these windows. I love the Hindu garden."

I may have not been very practiced, but I knew a romantic situation when I saw it handed to me. Rising from the bed, I padded in sock feet to stand by her. She laced my waist with her arm and drew me to kiss her. That woman knew how to kiss and also how to seduce. I never, in all our time together, cared to know how she got the experience. I was just glad her talents were showered on me.

Johanna, arms still wrapped around me, rose from my windowsill. She drew me tighter to her body with strong hands learning the feel of my back. I raised my arms to hug her neck and kissed her more. She was tall– taller than me. It was a new experience for me, and I liked it–her ability to encircle, to hold, to lead. I unclipped her barrette and that beautiful long black hair enfolded us. I loved its scent, her scent, the scent she evoked from me; her feel, her feel of me. The kisses grew from tentative to searching to passionate, and, suddenly the small room held much more heat than that given off by the radiator.

My hands searched her damp shirt, learning the curve of her back, the feel of her breast. I kissed the rivulet of sweat that formed in the hollow of her throat and worked to unbutton her shirt. Her hands held my waist, and she kissed my forehead.

Whispering, she said, "Diane, I usually undress myself–especially on a night like tonight."

"I'd love to do it. Please, let me," I whispered huskily as I pulled her shirttails from her jeans and slipped the shirt from her shoulders, letting it fall to the floor. Instinctively, she let me go, and I knelt to pick it up and put it on the chair. That moment on that night became an omen to me–of what she wanted and what she expected. This act–a symbolic kneeling adoration–jolted through me. She touched my shoulder as I was midway up from my kneeling position. That in actuality was what caused the physical jolt–her touch. It was gentle and commanding, but to me it was sensually magic.

"Diane, meine Liebchin, do stand up and take off your duds–slowly. I want to watch you." As she spoke, she slowly began to unbutton her jeans.

"I'm butch. Your watching me is not what I had in mind."

"I know, but, please . . ."

The "please" was way too seductive. How could I resist? I started with the shirt buttons then my bra. I squirmed out of them. My sweat made them cling to me like saran wrap to a cold bowl. I watched as she edged off her jeans and underwear. I hadn't a clue when her shoes had gone. I removed my jeans then my underwear and socks. I was thankful I didn't have to take the time to unlace my boots.

We stood facing each other . . . she–silhouetted in the moonlight through the windows . . . me–hidden in the room's shadows, which disguised my timidity and broken breathing.

She spoke first. "I must tell you something we didn't talk about."

"Yes?" I wondered that maybe the woman was a stone butch or perhaps she expected me to be one–which was far beyond my capacity tonight.

"I have a ritual."

"Oh," I reasoned out loud, but thought, "It's S/M. Now I'm in trouble, not technically knowing a cat-of-nine-tails from a whip."

"Nothing serious," she spoke as if she read my mind. "It's just that I'm a Hungarian witch."

I'm not worried about the witch part. You touch my soul already, I thought. I laughed and said, "Hungarian, is it–do you only make love with your native tongue–in your native tongue?"

She laughed, "I've never gotten quite that response before. You are all I knew you'd be." She laughed some more.

Our laughing broke the heat of the room with the familiarity of our selves . . . our alikeness, our passion.

With great solemnity, she spoke. "In the name of the Goddess, this night of the Great Full Moon, I come to you and give myself freely."

With that, she stepped the two steps between us and took me in her arms. I wanted that kiss I craved from her, but I am a lover of ritual and spoke first, "Isn't there something I should say?"

"You don't mind the ceremony?"

"Certainly not, it's you. I want to learn. I'm going to be a long-time lover." I said that so calmly, but was screaming inside for her kiss and her feel.

"Tonight," she whispered, as she graced my jaw-bone with soft, soft kisses, "the Goddess will be happy with just a little ditto."

"To the Goddess, I say ditto." I hurried the words as my hands held the breasts that my lips then kissed.

"That's one modern prayer, Sweetheart. I like it."

Johanna cradled me with soft, demanding arms and lay me on the bed. She kissed me with an authority that pulled my soul and my heart from me. Strong, capable hands found me wet and rocking. Her fingers became fish that swam up the stream of me. I clung to her as a child clings to a mother when it is afraid of falling from a terrible height. I clung to her as a passionate lover–leaving my nail marks on her back. She comforted me, gave me what I needed. She drove me to agony-to the point of sexual release . . . then backed away only to bring me to that point, more heightened, again and bring its fulfillment with an intensity I'd never known. It became that which I craved to know again, regardless of the cost or consequences. She sucked, she kissed, she bit, she soothed, she whispered, she laughed, she teased, then tortured and brought me to release. Johanna cast a spell over me that has made most other lovers inadequate. She was gentle, she was rough, she was in control–something I never, never gave up. Something, for the sake of her intimacy, I would never want again.

The heat of her, the heat of the room, mingled with our scents and desire. I could not get enough of her–her kiss, her tongue upon me, the feel of her beautiful ivory skin or that long hair which surrounded us both and became curlier and curlier, as she dripped sweat upon me.

Johanna brought my body release and pleasure, but her presence, her skilled actions eased me to a point more difficult to obtain–a point that set my mind free, a point of no time, no space, no worries, and no concern. That ability I bless her for, more than all her exquisite kisses upon me.

When I could take no more–me, usually insatiable–when she could give no more, that woman who could love for hours like a practiced priestess of the Goddess Ishtar's temple, when the sheets of the bed stuck to us and bound us closer in our lovers' embrace, when the heat of the room no longer compared to the heat created by us, she edged me to her and nestled my head on her shoulder. I circled her with my arms, afraid that this exquisite lover was only a vision of another nightmare. Her breathing slowed. My heart's pounding lessened. She traced my face with her fingers where she found tears on my cheeks.

"What's this? Not happy with the way you've been treated?"

"Of course I am–who wouldn't be." I hugged her closer and entwined her legs in mine. We fit perfectly. "I'm afraid I could never bring all those feelings out of you–I don't know how."

"That is what I will bring from you. It's there, hidden. I can feel it. I can sense it."

From that day on, she called me Cole in the outside world and Diane when we touched, when we loved. She's the only one who spoke my name truly seductively.

I confessed, "I've had a few lovers, but none in any remote way have done to me what you just made me feel."

"I know," she whispered to me as she brushed away the tears. "I love you in the witch's way."

"I don't know what that means, but I want to learn." To seal my statement of promise, I kissed her.

"It's to love with truly wild abandon, to give your heart and soul to your lover. A price most women won't pay. They opt for control." With these words she nestled against me and pulled my tangled hair from my shoulder. "Sleep. It's late . . . and I love holding you."

"No, I want to make love to you first."

"Not tonight. We've a lifetime waiting."

I had never been able to sleep a night through with a lover. Restless to be gone, to be solitary after lovemaking ended, always made me remove myself. It was not a trait that had endeared me to those I had dated. In the circumstance of the moment, I instinctively tensed my body.

Johanna felt it, and again I sensed she read my mind. "Relax. They'll be no running from me. I am what you so desperately desire. You touch my heart, Diane. You are my mirrored self, minus a little training, of course." The words were the truest I had ever heard, tinged with the hint of a tease. "Sleep, Sweetheart."

I nestled, I eased, I held her hand. She kept me from the demons of worry, and I drifted toward sleep.

I awoke in an empty bed. The twin bed suddenly felt expansive without her. My vision focused on Johanna, her back to the bed, dressed in shoes, jeans, and bra, rummaging quietly through my closet.

Without turning, she spoke, "Glad you're awake, Cole. Can you tell me where you've hidden that beautiful lavender shirt? I'd like to wear it."

"Left end, behind my blue jacket."

"Thanks . . . here it is." She slipped it off the hanger and swung it over her shoulders and deftly placed her arms in it. She turned to let me watch her button it, taking particular attention with the cuffs. She buttoned and tucked it in her jeans, gazing at me with a seductive smile.

"How are you feeling, Cole?"

"Great! No, alive."

"Good. Get a shower and dress. We're headed off this conformist campus to a day and night in which to taste the wicked sins of Tampa."

We both laughed.

Johanna said, "There's no one here to be in the bathroom. It's wonderful. C'mon. Hurry up."

I obliged, and our day began. That's a moment of memory I hold in my heart of her–my Hungarian gypsy. Tall, beautiful, seductive and happy. She, who possessed such beautiful eyes and strong, capable hands–wearing a simple pair of jeans and a flannel shirt with such style, such confidence, she truly became the center of attention of the dance club in Tampa, where we found more than a little sin. The women of the room–on the dance floor and at the bar–could not take their eyes off her. Johanna always said it was because of the beautiful shirt she wore. I said it was because she bewitched them.

III. Buttoning Up the Conclusion

That weekend in Tampa was the first of many for

Johanna and me. That winter in Lakeland, Florida, was the coldest on record. The night air was filled for weeks with the smoke of thousands of smudge pots that dotted the groves of the area. It was such a contrast of sensations. The days were cold, crisp and bright. The cold brought a blueness to the sky that I've never seen since (Maybe it was because I was in love). The deep blue turn-toward-evening sky was just the color of Johanna's eyes.

The nights were Gothic–enveloped in smudge pot smoke and shrouded in the terror of financial ruin. Almost every family of the area was linked to the citrus in some way. At night, I'd think I could hear all those prayers of supplication gliding through the sky on the cold night air. I felt a foreboding, though. Neither the God of the Methodist Church nor the Lady of the Moon was smiling.

As the weather remained unchanged, the mood of the daytime turned sinister. The local catastrophe, mixed with the tensions of war protests that were gaining all over the country, combined to produce an uneasiness, an unrest in our campus, its parents, students, and faculty.

On a cold Thursday afternoon in February, I was in my room finishing a paper for my Art History class. My perceptions took in the bustle, movement, and noise of the dorm, as well as the wind hitting my windows and rattling the panes ever so slightly. I pushed these distractions to the back of my mind. A bibliographic list and I would be finished. Concentration consumed me as I arranged the source cards in alphabetical order.

"Hey, Di, the Greek is downstairs. Says she'll stay five minutes. If you're here, open your window." My next-door neighbor, Sarah, spoke as she stuck her head in my door then moved quickly to her room.

Startled, I dropped the handful of cards and cursed under my breath. "Thanks," I yelled, so she could hear.

I went to the window and peered out. There she was all right–my Greek, my gypsy, my joy, my inspiration, my lover–she, who was turning my world and emotions upside down.

She was standing in the middle of the walkway that cut campus perpendicular to McDonald Avenue. It was filled with students coming and going . . . most with books, on this early afternoon. They walked in small groups and chatted as they took their time, even in the cold (Southern sauntering is an acquired art learned from childhood. We rarely give it up. You could tell the Northern kids. They always hurried on campus, even though the cold now upon us was nothing compared to their winters).

Johanna stared up at my windows, shadowing her eyes from the glint of the sun they reflected. When she saw me look out, she waved, dropped her hands to pantomime, with palms upraised, lifting the window open. I nodded and did as she demonstrated.

Sticking my head out, I yelled, "Hi! Cold enough for ya?" I rested my crossed arms on the windowsill with my chin on them and squatted with knees balancing against the wall. It was a pretty comfortable position, as long as I gazed at Johanna.

"Sure is! Don't you see my Aunt Genevieve's wool scarf around my neck?" She held up one end and dangled it. "Can't talk. Greek Council in an hour. Need a favor." Our intimate conversation was oblivious to those passing on the sidewalk. This scene was repeated a million times a day with those who were lucky enough to have side-walk windows.

"And that would be?"

She stood out from those around her. Dressed in black leather, knee-high boots, long herringbone wool dress coat cut in military fashion, and Aunt Genevieve's stylish white wool scarf, which made her gorgeous long hair look even darker in contrast. The only thing that kept her from being an advertisement for a Northern fashion photograph was the absence of hat and gloves. She was the exception–most students didn't own a true winter coat.

"Your lavender shirt. Will come up to get it, if it's okay. Can't stay. Meet me on the middle landing?"

"Sure, no problem. Be right there." As I closed the window I saw her move toward the side alcove door. I grabbed the shirt, hanger and all, and headed downstairs.

We met, almost simultaneously, on the landing. Quicker than the baton transfer in the Olympics, she had the shirt and was heading toward the front entrance that faced the Greek houses. There wasn't even a semblance of conversation. Her smile and my wink were enough. I watched her walk through the lobby filled with furniture that once graced a New York oil tycoon's mansion in the last century. Every chance I got, I watched her when she was unaware. She seemed to me, in those circumstances, her most seductive.

As her hand touched the huge wooden door, she turned (How did she know I would still be on those stairs?). "Remember, Cole, there's a rally at the President's house at 4:00 p.m. We need all the support we can get. Come and bring all those politically active, feminist friends of yours." She laughed and waved good-bye, turned to her intended route, and was swallowed by the sunlight, still holding the shirt hanger with her index finger.

I laughed. My friends on the third floor, left quad of Joseph Reynolds Dormitory for Freshmen Women, were not politically active or feminist. At this campus, it was a well-believed myth that Feminists were burned at the stake after midnight on the library commons.

I turned to go up the stairs and to the spilled index cards on my floor. My thoughts were with Johanna and my shirt. She hadn't worn it since our first date in Tampa, but I envisioned her in it this weekend, with the tight black pants I liked so much.

My friend, Sarah, met me on the stairs headed down. "What's up, Di?" Doing anything tonight? Want to go to study or to the student union?"

"Nothing much. Do you want to go to the Greek rally protesting dress codes? The President's house, 4:00 p.m. Johanna says they need all the support they can get."

"Sure! Anything for an adventure!" Her eyes twinkled. She was a Navy brat who lived on her chutzpah and life's uncertainties. I think her parents sent her to this conservative place to make her a more "Proper Lady."

"Meet you at 3:30. Steps of the Hindu garden?"

"Sure. See you then."

We parted. I spent the afternoon with the index cards.

I arrived at the steps 30 minutes early. The assignment finished, I had a sense of accomplishment and wanted to take a few minutes to breathe, to relax, and to soak in the winter day, which was still bitterly cold, but so stunning in its feel and so very unusual. I scrunched, in the heaviest coat I had, on the top step with my back to one of the two stone elephant sentries. It blocked the wind but kept me visible to the sidewalk for Sarah's arrival.

As I turned to view the garden, the most time-splitting déjà vu scene caught my eye. There, with students only fifty feet away, were eight Buddhist priests clad in saffron robes, sweaters, and sandals, admiring the Hindu temple and talking excitedly in some other-than-English language. Two were seated on stone benches by the reflecting pool and sketching on large drawing pads, as another pointed toward Annie Pfeiffer Chapel. His raised hands marked the lines and angles of our campus' most famous Frank Lloyd Wright architecture in broad strokes in the air. He would comment, and the two priests seated would nod agreement and sketch. He would wait until they finished, and the scene would repeat.

Captivated, startled, and curious, I watched them in silence. My history professor appeared from behind the trees on the garden cross path in front of the temple. His hands were stuck deep in the pockets of a new Florida Southern College red and white windbreaker, which was zipped to the knot in his navy blue tie.

When Dr. Gordon saw me, he headed for the garden steps. "Ms. Cole, you are fine today, I hope."

"Yes, sir . . . but not used to seeing priests in the temple."

We laughed. What irony. It was the one place most given to them in any historical context.

"Students of architecture from Tibet and Rani, India. I'm the official campus tour guide. Several converse in the Queen's English better than I."

Dr. Gordon was tall, thin, intellectual, suave, and possessed a deadly wit. He was an anachronism in time—truly more given to the literary salons of 18th century

France than contemporary America. I grew to admire, respect, and emulate his historical ethics and philosophies in the four years I studied under him. He was one of the few intellectual historians (in the degreed sense) I ever met.

He glanced at his watch. "Three-thirty. Must get my charges to the President's house by four. We're having coffee and the newspapers, local PBS station and Tampa TV are coming for interviews. Good day."

"See you, sir."

Gathering up the group, Dr. Gordon turned right on the cross path. The President's home faced Lake Hollingsworth on the edge of campus, less than two hundred yards from where we stood. Buffered by a rolling, grassy hill and centuries-old oaks, it was barely visible to the modern architecture, which contrasted to its Southern antebellum style. It was a true high plantation home surrounded by academia and a modern city street instead of orange groves.

I watched as the last saffron robe disappeared into the thick vegetation of the garden. Daydreaming of India and the mystery of its cultures and peoples, I was brought to reality by Sarah's soft tap on my head.

"Di, did you hear? The Greeks are planning a *big* rally. Everyone able will be there! Frats to support their little sisters on the Council and sororities vice versa. Let's go. I want a good ringside seat!"

Sarah helped me up and suddenly I realized that the walkway behind me held more people than I'd ever seen on it. The campus was predominantly Greek, and they were out in force. Greek jerseys and house banners were everywhere. There was a tide of people flowing toward the red brick home of the President. I thought about the priests. I didn't think the President was expecting all of us for coffee.

The walkway that the tide was taking led through Polk Science (it's in the Frank Lloyd Wright design; the walk literally cuts the science department in half.), around the auditorium and down the far side of the grassy hill, ending at the back of the President's home. Dr. Gordon took the straight route. This assemblage, almost five hundred by now, would take longer to get there.

I felt closed in and crowded and pulled Sarah from the walkway to the garden steps. "Let's cut across the hill. Stay out of the crowd, okay?"

By this time, the FSC Music Department was marching by (in precise formation) and giving a rousing rendition of the "Alma Mater." People cheered, clapped and whistled for more.

Maybe it was the weather, maybe what Dr. Gordon would term the Zeitgeist, or maybe it was way too many Greeks with too much time on their hands–but this afternoon was getting a little weird. Conservatism and restraint were out the window by the time the bulk of the throng hit Polk Science. You could feel that protest had become the vogue. Vent-up protest for a number of campus and non-campus complaints wrapped itself in the guise of FSC's dress code.

Sarah and I made record time in getting to the top of the hill. We could hear the shouting, cheering and general whoopla. We saw that the crowd was halfway to the auditorium and gathering people from the library commons and Ordway Arts–the FLW building which held Social Sciences, Psych, and Languages, both the classrooms and offices.

We settled onto the top of the hill with the sun warming us and the breeze from Lake Hollingsworth dying to a sudden calm. Patiently we waited for what Sarah termed "excitement" to happen, and, believe me, we were not disappointed. Our view was absolutely spectacular for what was to follow.

"All we need, Di, is some popcorn and a couple cans of cold beer."

"That's a suspension on this campus," I said as I watched the maze of color and sound weave its way past the auditorium.

"Yeah, I know, but it's too big a price to pay for some dry-cooked corn," Sarah blurted out, and slapped me on the back. We hooted and giggled.

"Think this sideshow can get any more exciting?" Sarah asked, as her eyes swept the throng, still weaving and growing.

Glancing to my left, I responded as dryly as I could, "Sure do—in more ways than one." I pointed to Lake Hollingsworth Drive and the sorority houses that faced it. More precisely, I pointed to the paved roadway that ran behind the Greek houses.

That's when we saw the military maneuvers. Eighty dressed ready-for-combat soldiers practicing combat line skills behind the sorority houses, weaving in and out of the ligustrum hedges, ducking behind garbage dumpsters, slithering between bicycle racks and the FLW architecture, and taking up positions behind parked VWs. A lieutenant was giving silent hand signals to spread out and charge the retaining wall, which was at the edge of the grassy hill that sloped into the President's backyard, where we could see eight yellow robes and two suited males having coffee on the glassed-in porch.

Now, FSC was big into ROTC, and all freshmen men were required to participate. Thursday afternoons were overtaken by maneuver classes, and you sort of got resigned to GI Joes leaping unannounced upon you. Students even participated. We could suddenly be "ambushed" coming out of a building or walking across campus. The ladies of the Greek persuasion were known to position themselves at ambush-frequented spots in the esplanades to be able to surrender news of an upcoming party to the best-looking platoon.

Every once in a while the soldiers would storm the President's home, for effect. The military leadership of the ROTC department liked to show their readiness and capability. Today, President Donahue would get a personal demonstration of their military preparedness.

The gravity of the situation was hitting us both. Seriousness struck us like lightning.

All Sarah could say was, "Oh, my God." She put her hands over her face and spread her fingers slightly to look. "Is that what I think it is?"

"Sure is," was all I could reply.

"I didn't know Lakeland had so much media," she gasped.

Those words ended as we watched three logo-emblazoned media vehicles pull up in front of the President's side yard. Cameramen began pulling out equipment and scattering tripods and lights around the back porch. A well-dressed lady, briefcase in hand, headed toward the door.

"How long till the soldiers get there?"

"Four to five minutes," I conjectured. "Just about

the time the mob makes the trees on the other side of the back yard."

Now, don't think that everyone wasn't noticing the thunderous noise from the Greeks. Dean Wynarski and six campus security guards ran past us from behind, while everyone else was converging with destiny. They had taken our path through the Hindu garden. At forty-two, Dean Wynarski was a good twenty years younger than the youngest member of the security team and sprinted a little faster. He made President Donahue's back door at the same instant as the brief-case lady. The six security gentlemen stopped all around us to catch their breaths. Most took out back pocket handkerchiefs to wipe sweat on this cold day, then slowly walked down the hill. They didn't take their eyes off Dean Wynarski and were about mid-field when all concerned (big groups of people, that is) broke through the trees or jumped the retaining wall, with rifles positioned for warfare.

Some say time doesn't go in slow motion to provide a more intense life experience. Truly, I can say that it does. Six elderly guards were shocked, stunned, and surrounded on the left by soldiers who were putting on their best performance for President Donahue and their commanding officers. Every rifle had them in their line of fire. On the right, about six hundred fifty rowdy Greeks broke through the trees, chanting a Pi Kappa Alpha drinking song, while the percussion section of the band beat out its rhythm. Everyone sang along. Greeks believed it was the most indecent, immodest, and societally improper drinking song on campus. Everyone knew it and wished their particular group had written it. Banners were raised up and down to accompany the rhythm. Sorority sisters did a jaunty two-step with raised and lowered arm movements to the catchy chant. It looked, from our vantage point, that more than a few could really "cut a rug." Fraternity brothers clapped and sang boisterously.

I think Sarah and I both prayed silently that the security guards would not keel over.

Surprisingly, above the din, we heard the well-dressed woman scream, "Are you getting tape on this? I want still photos, too! Now, this is a protest march! That audio better be on or heads will roll."

Sarah was speechless5which is saying a great deal in a few words. I was dumbfounded. It was like viewing a Peter Max poster after having dropped way too much acid. The only movement between us to acknowledge this scene was Sarah removing her hands from her face to get a better view.

Suddenly, the unexpectedness of everything hit everybody. As President Donahue emerged from the back of the house, holding the door himself for eight robed monks, one history professor and twelve Greek Council members, which included Johanna, the crowd hurrahed and cheered and turned toward the house. The surrealism wasn't quite complete–a dozen or so cars on Lake Hollingsworth Drive stopped traffic both ways, as drivers got out of their vehicles to mingle with the fringes of the military group, who had lowered their rifles.

I watched the mingling and laughing and heard a little more music. Everyone was waiting for something. This was such an event . . . or should I say spectacle? Spectacle is the right word. In nonviolent protest, every member of the Greek Council had worn something not allowed in the dress code handbook. Most opted for a single piece of contraband clothing, such as walking shorts or ill-fitting bell bottoms (The walking-shorts people had sported knee socks due to the climatic conditions).

As President of the Greeks, Johanna raised her hand for silence and, to my amazement, got it. She gave a great speech on student dress code demands and explained to all that everything she visibly had on was considered improper–men's oxfords, khakis, belt, shirt and tie. She said she wore them willingly in protest. Any punishment President Donahue handed out would be fine with her.

The crowd stayed quiet as she presented the written demands to President Donahue. Eight monks looked at him earnestly and waited for a reply. Dr. Gordon gave him his full attention and smiled. The media lady held a microphone to catch his words. Dean Wynarski handed him a megaphone, which he had retrieved from the trunk of our school's only security vehicle that had arrived in time to miss the traffic jam.

President Donahue was a great, personable man. A Southern gentleman and scholar from the Old School. He knew every student by name. Today he would be considered a true Orville Reddenbacher type–he even wore a bow tie. Acknowledging the legitimacy of the demands, he said he would speak the next morning to the Foundation membership. He introduced the monks from Tibet and India; though some of the names were a little difficult to pronounce, he used no written notes. Explaining that they were here for an architectural study of Mr. Frank Lloyd Wright's buildings, he welcomed them to our campus and said that he spoke for the students and faculty when he said that our campus was open to them for the week and everyone would do their best to make their visit as pleasant as possible.

We clapped and cheered. The monks smiled and waved.

The media lady was having a field day. She had photos snapped of the monks and Greek Council together. Now, I can tell you that was some kind of visual juxtaposition. Not to lose the moment, or a crowd, President Donahue turned to Johanna and asked what punishment would be appropriate. As a true satyagrahist (nonviolent protestor), she said nothing, but continued to keep his gaze. The crowd waited in anticipation. Everyone knew a symbolic punishment would be forthcoming. The stillness was broken by a monk, who stepped forward and conversed several minutes with the President in private low tones. He bent his head close to the President's ear, and we all waited and watched. President Donahue nodded in agreement on several occasions and, when the monk had finished conversing with him, handed him the megaphone and stepped back.

Surveying the crowd, the monk calmly spoke, "President Michael A. Donahue, Ph.D. and leader of your academic institution, has agreed that this young lady is as guilty as my brethren and I are of breaking your established dress code rules for this campus." He paused and patted his robes. "We're sure this isn't listed as proper attire in your handbook."

Everyone cheered, whistled, clapped and nodded heads in agreement.

The monk waited for silence then continued. "In his wisdom, and feeling the justice of your cause, President Donahue has granted us—and your Greek

Council–the pleasure of having dinner tomorrow at his home, as penalty for our nonviolent actions toward established rules."

The crowd truly exploded. Everyone cheered, screamed, jumped up and down and let out FSC war whoops only used at soccer games. Soldiers patted security guards on the back, sorority sisters kissed their significant others in public, frat brothers embraced and gave secret handshakes (no one was looking, so it was pretty safe to do so). Dr. Gordon and President Donahue shook hands with the monks, who gave the crowd the clasped hands signal for winning above their heads or peace signs, while the media lady was orchestrating which shots for the cameramen to get. Band members struck up "Happy Days Are Here Again" in very perky time.

Every Greek, non-Greek, every faculty member and employee of the college in that group knew that things would change–a change that was a very long time in coming; but a change that the next year would embolden the Greek Council to take on Saturday classes.

Sarah and I hugged and whooped along with the crowd. "Now that's some damn excitement!" she screamed as we danced around. I waved and waved with both hands and jumped up and down. Johanna searched the crowd till she found me and waved back and tugged at the lavender shirt.

After a speech by Dean Wynarski to leave in an orderly way, the crowd began to disassemble. From our vantage point, my friend and I watched the activity and the camera crew taking shots of everything. The media lady, microphone in hand, cornered the Greek Council. A few members of the Music Department sat on the grass in a circle and played Peter, Paul and Mary's "Blowin' in the Wind." Sarah and I agreed that the song fit both the situation and the weather. Most everyone, still in a lively mood, headed for the cafeteria. The school was so small that everyone usually ate at the same time.

Sarah and I walked to supper, taking the route back through the Hindu garden.

When spring break came a month later, I spent a lot of evenings on the dock thinking about the day of the protest. It was the talk of the campus and Lakeland for weeks afterward. By the time the rumors began and the retelling started, the protest became THE PROTEST. To folks in Lakeland to this day, it was to protest the war. Why else would Buddhist monks be in a picture with President Donahue and members of the Greek Council? Actually, the paper printed a front page article with three huge pictures;–one taken from the top of the camera truck, which showed the mass of students waving banners looking like they were being surrounded by rifle-waving soldiers (The media lady's article had an anti-war flair; it quoted the Buddhists on a wide range of issues). President Donahue, flanked by Buddhist monks, the Greek Council and Dr. Gordon, was the subject of the second picture. The last picture showed a half-body shot of Johanna handing the demands to President Donahue, with a kindly monk smiling at her side.

This was the picture I pulled out of my knapsack and showed my Mother and Godmother as we sat on our front porch after dinner. My Mom was honored that her handwork made the "Lakeland Ledger's" front page. She later made a copy to show the women of her weekly coffee club.

My Godmother studied the picture carefully then looked directly at me. "The young woman wearing the shirt is beautiful. Is she in your dorm?"

"No, Ma'am," I replied. "She's my friend, but a Greek who lives on the other side of the campus."

"Is she as smart, bright, well-mannered and as quiet as you?"

"Three out of four," I replied. "She's talkative but also a very good listener."

"Then, Diane, I think she's someone worth walking across campus to get to know better. Am I right?"

"Yes, Ma'am," I answered and smiled. My God-mother knew my heart.

Years later, she heard about the great brouhaha from Johanna, who was wearing the beautiful lavender shirt, as I held both their hands.

Chapter Four

Running For My Life

It is a spring day in Florida. The humidity and heat of summer are a good six weeks away. A calm, cool morning is filtering shafts of sunlight through the sprouting growth of oaks and pines. Birds that dart through the branches are noisily announcing the locations of foraging squirrels. Intricate spider webs nestled between palmettos and wild blackberry bushes are prism struck with the drops of morning dew. The North Florida landscape of the state park I'm in is underpopulated, pristine, picture perfect—and I'm running for my life.

Why I notice the details of the scenery clipping past me is a force of habit—a historian's attention to detail that through practice and reuse has become an obsessive part of my personality. Now, it is a trait that focuses my mind, even while I jump a small fallen pine log that lies across the trail I run upon. I turn my head slightly to check my peripheral vision for my pursuer and gulp for more air, while I do not diminish my pace. Breathing has become a problem–historians don't run a great deal professionally.

I can't see my pursuer, but I hear the chatter of upset birds back behind my left shoulder and hear rustles through the underbrush. The distance between that noise and myself has not shortened since mentally checking about one hundred fifty feet back. As my T-shirt becomes soaked across my back and stomach and I pull for more and more air with red-hot lungs, I must concentrate. I must devise a plan to escape capture, because I can't continue running at this pace much longer.

Hitting a level part of the path in an open break of the woods, with about fifteen hundred feet to the next stand of trees, I clench my fists and pump my arms for momentum, as I run with all the proper mechanics I can remember from high school gym class. Sweat pouring even in the early morning, breaths that do not fill my lungs and tightening muscles screaming to stop, make me wish I'd paid more attention to Mrs. Parnelli and fourth period P.E. My tennis shoes dig into the gravel path that heads for the woods. The crunch of gravel will readily give away my position, but I'm sure my very audible gasps for air have already done that. I concentrate, remove blurring scenery distractions from my mind and do what my Dad always said to do in a desperate circumstance–focus, look for options, and keep calm. I think about my Dad, run like hell toward the tree line ahead and try to devise a plan.

Making the stand of trees, I am blessed with cool morning shadows created by the canopy of foliage. Listening carefully, I don't hear any nearby steps of my pursuer. I've grown up in woods of this kind and hope that bit of luck will be my salvation. I slip from the path, turn right toward a small rise in the terrain and try to control my gasping breaths. My salvation will be my silence. One hundred feet farther and at the top of the small rise, I crouch and walk slowly, silently, through the underbrush. As I scoot over the rise, nestle into cold pine needles and press my body to the far side of the largest, closest pine at hand, I hear the gravel crunch with the rhythmic pounding of my pursuer's race steps. They sound measured and timed. Not like someone struggling for breath. Not like me, trying to take silent gulps while holding my spasmodic stomach muscles with fists pushed into my gut.

The path, turned from hard stone to fallen tree leaves, will make keeping track of my pursuer harder. As I nestle as close to the tree as possible and feel the shingle-layered bark prickle through my shirt, I pull my knees to my stomach to quiet my muscles and diminish my occupied space. I'm hoping my pursuer is now ahead of me in this desperate chase.

The stand of trees has become naturally quiet. Only swooping birds and a fish hawk's cry break the stillness. A whispering breeze at the tops of the tall pines sets their tops to swaying. I watch their hypnotic, graceful dance as I raise my chin and wipe my neck with the bottom of my sweat-soaked shirt. The morning is growing late. Shafts of sunlight filtering down toward my face are becoming warmer and stronger. My breathing slows as I lean my head back to the tree. The filtering warmth eases my shoulder muscles. I silently stretch out my legs and point my toes. Closing my eyes to take in the calm of the moment and the warmth of the day that is soothing me, I feel I might possibly be able to survive this situation.

Listening, I hear no pursuer, no rustling or snapping of a giveaway sign. In a moment, as quickly as the sun falls from the treetops to my face, I survey the situation that has brought me to this plight of desperation, replaying in my mind how a misspoken word can make you run for your life.

We'd started our journey early. Very early. Johanna liked to see the sun come up over the lake. It was our ritual of spring–the Equinox of new beginnings. We celebrated every Wiccan holiday, but I believe this was her favorite. She said it reminded her of Easter as a little girl. Sunrise services with the words of new life, new hope.

Every year we'd bring our coffee and sandwiches, prepared at the diner five miles down the road; spread our blankets under majestic oaks that held our favorite view of the sunrise, and sit close to each other, cross-legged on the blankets, our hands intertwined. It was ritual; a moment that is crystal clear in my memory, unlike many mundane days of the year.

Chanting unwhispered prayers in our minds of togetherness, we watched and waited as the chilled, dark Florida night gave way to the dawn of equal day and equal night. It was miraculous and awe-inspiring. As fingers of light-pink, yellow and ice blue climbed ahead of the sun, Johanna's hand would tighten in mine. I always felt that the first glow of the sun sparked her heart with enough love to enfold me for millennia. That she was a daughter of the Goddess was always evident to me, as I would always at this most loved moment, study her blue eyes that mirrored this magnificent dawn. That studious glance showed me my true Johanna. She had eyes that set my soul and heart ablaze with one beckoning look. One sly wink could make me melt into their sapphire blueness in a breath's moment.

We'd greet this day in our ritual of meditation and silence. When the whole sun rode above the treetops of the lake's edge and the day was truly alive, we'd kiss and give our blessing to each other for Eostra's Day. We'd partake of our bagged breakfasts and linger in our favorite spot as long as time permitted.

This year, we lingered in lazy idleness . . . both having the next three days off. We sipped our coffee and reveled in the certain beauty of the day. I leaned with my back against an oak. Johanna nestled between my chest and propped-up knee. She held her coffee in one hand, wrapped her other arm around my knee and gazed across the lake. When she was this close, this enticing, my heart always had my mind and body tense with excitement for her. Such beauty, that the sadness of circumstance had not yet marred, begged to be touched, to be kissed.

I placed a kiss on the nape of her neck, just behind her ear and whispered, "You know I can't do without you. You're my life."

She turned and smiled and kissed me, full-mouthed. My body was warmed by the sun of Johanna's being.

"But you . . . you could," she whispered into my ear.

"You want to bet? You're on. I love your challenges."

I sat my coffee on the grass, then Johanna's. She hopped up and held out her hand to help me. Always the properly attired lecturer, she smoothed her pants and shirt. We faced off. I knew it wouldn't be arm-wrestling. I always won those contests.

Hands on hips, she stared me up and down, then beyond me, across the lake, to compose the most devilish challenge she could muster. Usually our challenge rate was about fifty-fifty. I always picked something I knew she was capable of winning. She fulfilled my dyke-self by setting her tasks just hard enough for me to struggle with, but able to accomplish. I figured that today it might be stone-throwing across the lake. I figured wrong.

"A race."

"Okay with me," I casually replied.

"A race–around the lake."

"And if you win?" I queried.

She said the words slowly, with the calculated manner of a trial lawyer giving opening statements. "I'll give you a head start. If I catch you, Diane, there will be a month of no touching, no kisses, no nights of my warm body on yours–no sex."

"Are you serious? C'mon."

"As serious as hell, my dear. You just said you couldn't do without me. Believe me, you're running for my life, your life, our life, for the next month . . . and be certain, Diane, I'll run in earnest to catch you."

"Why? Why this terrible wager?" I asked with tears in my eyes. We never backed down from a dare.

"Because I know you love me and will give it your all. I'm running out of dares to suit you. If you win–which you won't–no wagers for a year. I want to find something you won't do to prove your love for me. I want to break that spirit of yours–just a little. I love you so much, I guess I just want to see how far you'll go for me."

A dare was a dare and we never, ever admitted defeat. Facing her, sweat mingling with the uncertainty of the outcome on my upper lip, I smiled and questioned in my most seductive voice, "Okey-dokey. A kiss for good luck before we begin?"

She had to smile. "Sure."

That kiss was no peck on the cheek. She poured all into it that I would miss for a month if I lost. That symbol of good luck made me determined that I would not lose.

Johanna shooed me down the path with a wave of her hand and yelled, "I'll start when you pass the first picnic bench."

I nodded in agreement and took off in earnest. About four hundred yards was not a big lead, but I calculated to run with all my might and lengthen my advantage.

My plan had worked until now. My darling was deadly persistent in anything she set her mind to. I knew now, as I took my first few decent breaths in a while, as I leaned against the tree and felt the day warm, she was hell-bent on catching me.

Listening carefully, I slowly scrunched over the hill rise, through the underbrush and cautiously began to jog down the trail. I now know why deer constantly perk their ears while feeding. Danger could creep up swiftly on a leaf-softened path. Nothing in view. A tad of confidence crept in, and I quickened my pace.

A few minutes of slow running brought two

approaching figures into view. I figured Johanna was far ahead of me. The elderly couple on a leisurely walk around the lake sported all the tell-tale signs of non-native Floridians—snowwhite limbs poked out of short-sleeved shirts and walking shorts, wide-brimmed Panamas that sported tiny maple leafs on the hat bands, and a dangling, expensive camera around the gentleman's neck.

When I was almost upon them, I raised a hand and gave a "hi." They stopped, with worried looks. An upheld hand of the woman beckoned me to halt. "Are you alright, dear? You look, well, disheveled."

I suddenly realized I surely must seem so. Climbing on knees and hands over the hill rise, sitting my butt in pine needles and dirt, whelped scratches forming on my arms from slinking through the underbrush, plus a gallon of sweat soaked into my hair and clothes, probably qualified me for first-rate dishevelment.

Stopping, as requested, I tried to become a little presentable by wiping the grime from my forearms. "Just fine, ma'am. Just jogging with my friend."

The gentleman offered his clean, folded, back-pocket bandana. I took it, wiped my face (which probably looked like my forearms), and nodded my appreciation for his gesture.

"That's more sweat than the ordinary jog. You've been running, little lady."

"Yes, sir," I agreed and mentally added "for my life."

"Dear, not to be imposing, but would your friend be the beautiful young woman sitting at the picnic area we just passed?"

I had to be a tad careful. Johanna could have baited a ploy with this most sincere couple. "Probably so, ma'am." I was cool.

"Do hope everything is okay with her. What a coincidence. Just gave her my hanky–she was crying. Now Stephen has given you his."

It was no ploy. Johanna didn't cry or give the pretense of crying for anyone. I was worried now. My eyes and demeanor showed it.

"Best be on your way, dear. Keep Stephen's handkerchief. He packed a dozen for this trip."

"Yes. Thanks . . . for the information and the bandana." I tied the bandana around my neck as I began running in earnest down the path. I was intent in my purpose and discontent at my Johanna's crying. Was she hurt? Was she sick? What had brought her such despair? I had a plan for winning the wager, but now that seemed so unimportant, so trivial. I could withstand a month of celibacy and defeat. The distance to the picnic area was made in record time. I stopped at the edge of the stand of trees, bent to catch my breath as I rested my hands on my upper legs, and scanned the area for Johanna.

She sat on top of a picnic table, feet resting on the seat bench, her hands covering her lowered face. I felt like running pell-mell to her, but something in me made me hold my stride to a silent walk.

I kept my eyes on her. No crying now. She lifted her face to look over the lake view and to wipe her eyes on a delicate, white handkerchief. My diagonal path brought me toward the back of her left shoulder. Lost in thought and wiping already-shed tears that glistened from her cheeks, she didn't notice my approach.

Three feet from the opposite side of the picnic table, I stepped onto the other bench and, with one blended motion, cupped her shoulder with my hand.

She turned, startled, and smiled. I climbed over the tabletop, put my arm around her shoulder, squeezed her softly, and sat close beside her.

"Well, Diane, my dearest, you've caught me. You win." She smiled through more falling tears and hugged me, while planting a soft, seductive kiss on my cheek. I hugged back and gulped for air to replenish lungs that weren't really over the first sprint to the stand of trees or concerns for the love of my life.

"Are you okay? The folks on the trail said you were crying. Do you hurt? Do you need the paramedics?" I tried to question lightly, but now the tears slid down my cheeks. She cupped her hands and brushed the tears from my face. Both our handkerchiefs were soaked and beyond their utilitarian purpose.

"Fine, love . . . but feeling stupid."

"Sure you're really okay?"

Johanna held my hand and pulled pine needles from my T- shirt. She looked me up and down. "You are a mess. What happened to you?"

"My sneak plan to ambush you from behind. Not very well executed, I'm afraid." I looked down at the mess I truly was and nervously tied a loose shoestring.

"Please, J, why the tears?"

"I ask you to do the craziest things–and you do. Do you love me that much? I find it so hard to believe."

I entwined my very grimy fingers in her slender, perfectly manicured ones and felt the spark of electricity that forged through my body and heart whenever I touched her. "J, I'm so devoted to you, so lost in my love for you, that I would run for my life with you to the end of the earth."

She ran her free fingers through my hair, removing an errant blade or two of leatherleaf fern. Smiling, truly happy and content, she kissed me. For that kiss, all the physical and emotional pain of the morning was gladly endured.

"Just one question, J. How in the hell did you keep up such a pace for so long?"

She laughed that wicked, seductive chuckle that melted my heart. "Diane, I ran like that because I was *determined* to win. All those summers of tennis lessons paid off in stronger legs than I thought I had. Guess a girl from the 'burbs can hold her own with you country girls any day, eh?"

"You sure can," I agreed. "You're so full of surprises. I'll never know all of you in this lifetime."

"Well, we've all the time in a long life for that," she said and kissed me again.

That night as Johanna nestled in my arms, we agreed to no wagers or dares for a year. As she held me protectively, comforted and safe for the rest of the night, I dreamed of chasing a beautiful, strong Amazon with Johanna's eyes and hair, through the ruins of an ancient Greek temple. I won the chase. A bargain struck for a night of love with her under the great full moon was paid by my Amazon Queen with the sapphire blue eyes. As her mirrored self in my dream, Johanna's soft whispers and sensuous laugh brought smiles upon us from the Lady in the Moon.

For a while (no for a very long time, to be exact) I ran for no reason--not to catch a waiting elevator when late on an academic schedule or even to get out of a sudden downpour that haunted the summer days of the Florida State University campus.

I had run for my life, her life, our life, and won. That was enough for which to be grateful to the Goddess.

Chapter Five

A Nap On The Porch

It's a cold, rainy, sullen autumn day today in Northeast Florida. You know the kind of day I mean, even if you're from the Midwest or New York City. That day that sort of forces your world to slow just a little. A day that draws the emotional out of you instead of the practical. A day meant for curling up with a long-forsaken book, while you wear your favorite pair of beat-up, tatty socks and frayed sweat clothes. A day that may make your heart truly look at what it is longing for.

There are so many blessings in my life, so much possibility and joy, that were not there a few months ago, that I am very satisfied with the path this stage of my life seems to be heading toward. A day like today never fails to pull from the depths of my heart the sadness I carry for what has been lost to me. Sometimes I think it is the loss of my true self that I mourn. Sometimes I think what I mourn is the loss of first true love. Sometimes, my innocence. Sometimes, it's the passion and true devotion she inspired and coaxed from me . . . but mostly, today, I mourn the loss of my best friend, my most exquisite lover, my kindred sister.

The sound of the rain hitting the metal roof on my house hauntingly echoes the sound of the rain hitting the tin roof on Johanna's tiny, wood-frame bungalow of more than twenty-five years ago. I am drawn to the feel of us laying on a futon couch on her front porch. It was covered with her grandmother's handmade quilt. To make the futon a little softer, it was stuffed at both ends with throw pillows collected from every dorm room she or I had inhabited. All was covered over with a '50s Indian blanket that had graced my bed when I was growing up.

I always thought that couch mirrored Johanna's and my life. All our most cherished material possessions combined together to create a wonderfulness of practicality and comfort.

As I lay with her at my side, her arm propped up on the futon side rail on a soft throw pillow, almost cradling me in that lounging gesture, I closed my eyes and took in the exquisiteness of the moment that surrounded me—her feel, her perfume, her hand as she rubbed my shoulder in time to raindrops falling from the roof edge, our legs entwined in a dance of dungaree and thin, thin woolen tweed. Our stability and certainty of the moment reassured by intertwined-socked feet that were resting in their most favorite positions.

I could feel the slow rhythmic beating of her heart

and had the tantalizingly sexual feel of her long hair on my cheek. Johanna only unbound her hair for what she considered private, shared moments. Now those moments could be for everyone to enjoy, as in dinner out or a movie. I knew that flowing wild hair that caught the admiring eye of the gentlemen and blond, thin, flower-child types was, in those most public times, meant only for me. Today, it was unbound, with no intended public display. It was for my feel, my touch, my floating-in delight, as it now casually graced my cheek.

I kept my eyes closed and nestled with a small, contented sigh, into her. The rain cloaked our porch and lovers' bed with increased tempo and density, blocking out all concern, all worry, all that which would have to be done.

Slipping my hand beneath the edge of the Indian blanket, I lightly felt the threadwork of the quilt. It was such a beautiful expression of art, a fashioned piece of Johanna's life before she was in it–scraps of cloth worn from Eastern Europe, as her years-later-to-be Grandmother and Mother fled another war, another uprising. It would divest them of most material goods, except the expensive jewelry, loose gemstones, and a few Swiss account books, folded into coat hems and dress pockets and sewn with double-tight buttonhole stitches to secure their safety. I always thought this a reason Johanna was so the center of attention. Her kinswomen had had to be so unobvious, so blendable with the tragedy and circumstances around them.

The quilt also held Johanna's younger life . . . her much lived life before me. Pieces of checked gingham that were once sundresses, cherished squares of her flannel baby blankets, seersucker patches of a third-grade dress she absolutely adored, and a few small remnants of her favorite bear, worn to death by the love of her handling. The soles of his feet (the most salvageable portion of his anatomy) were donated to the production of the quilt, before he was given a solemn burial. Johanna dictated to her Mother the eulogy for the ceremony, which her Mom then read with reverence and heartfelt sympathy for the loss of a beloved member of the family. Given her predilection for those things Eastern at such an early age, Mr. Bear was cast, by Johanna's Dad, upon a funeral pyre in the garden of their yard. Mr. B's ashes were spread at a later day, by the gardener, around oak trees that Johanna loved to climb.

My fingers could feel the threads of a family history, as I blindly, gently examined the section of the quilt that was within reach of my touch. In my estimation, the most beautiful of all the triangles and squares lay beyond my reach, in the star center of the quilt. There were pieces of Johanna's Dad's silk tie and her Mother's silk vest worn on their wedding day. No traditional conventionality floated through Johanna's blood. Her parents held in their hearts a bit of the Bohemian, the exotic, the unexpected, that brought flourish and panache to life. I loved them for this genetic gift they gave to Johanna. I loved that she personified their joy of the now, the everyday, the everyway, with what seemed to be their intensity double fold. What I shut out of my heart, as I kept my eyes closed and focused on the loveliness of the quilt beneath me, was the feeling that seeped into the edges of my rationality, that such intensity might nullify a life of moderation that usually leads to longevity.

That was not something that concerned my young heart at the moment. What I felt was happiness, contentment, mirrored recognizability. I thought that would be enough to take us through forever.

A touch of breeze brought the raindrops onto the edge of the porch–but not close enough to disturb our quietness, our time that I wished would go on forever. I opened my eyes to watch the grayness of the afternoon sink deep into the sky of approaching evening. I listened to my heart, Johanna's heart, our breathing that was soft and content, like the children who could have worn the checked gingham sundresses of the quilt, resting in each other's arms, as they napped in the lazy afternoon after spending the morning climbing the oak trees of Johanna's garden.

Johanna stirred a tad and rested her hand on my dungareed hip. Her touch was so gentle at first it was hardly noticeable, but then those practiced fingers traced my thigh and pressed themselves with such sweetness into the feel of my muscle that I squirmed–just a little.

It was enough to evoke her sultry, low laugh. She whispered into my ear, "You know, my deary dumpling, we could, for once, unfold this futon and get under the quilt. I've plans for us." She grabbed the button waist of my dungarees and tugged to bring her point home.

I fidgeted and turned to her, face to face, breast to breast, thigh to thigh. Only our intertwined socks and my hand on her hip belied the mock seriousness of my voice. "And those would be?" I implored.

"Whatever fantasy you choose."

I kissed her and tried with every purposeful move I knew to mesh the molecules of our bodies together. For that smidgen of total nearness I could not attain, her hand in the small of my back accomplished.

"I want the true story of the checked gingham squares."

"You want what?" she giggled. "You mean the quilt squares? Not what I had in mind, Diane. I wanted a sex-filled night of passion with you."

"Please, dear J, combine both. I want the story of the squares."

"You are too weird. All that history research is definitely getting to you."

She climbed over me and helped me from the futon as she shook her head in exasperation.

I knew in my heart of hearts she would give me what I asked for. She always gave that, and more. She always got from me more than I thought it was humanly possible for me to possess. This night would be no different.

As the raindrops slowed to nothingness and the moon shone through the window of the bedroom, Johanna held me spellbound in the story of the gingham checks. Our skin was warm and smooth against each other, our lovers' sweat still visible in the moonlight as it slightly curled the wisps of Johanna's unbound hair and fell from my cheek onto the pillow.

I learned of a friend who held her heart at seven and made her want something more that she could not even name. To hear Johanna tell of her life before me always made me feel that a wider ocean was being created to hold the drops of our love brought forth with her words.

Holding her tight, I watched those beautiful blue eyes sparkle in the moonlight and that gorgeous smile reappear again and again, as she recalled a memory, nearly forgotten, that I jogged into reality with my request.

When her story ended, I kissed her in thanks. Our bodies were cool to the touch in the autumn night air. I pulled the quilt from the bottom of the bed to cover us and nestled into her waiting arms. That night we slept, soft and content, like the children who could have worn the checked gingham sundresses, resting in each other's arms, dreaming of lazy, sun-filled afternoons and the tall oaks, perfect for climbing, that graced Johanna's garden.

Chapter Six

Visual Addiction

I.

We all have a part of us that stays hidden, undiscussed–even with our best friend. I've never been one to pry into that area of my best friend's personality. Probably never will do so in the future. I believe some things are best kept undisclosed, but as I sit in the overstuffed, comfortable chair in my lover's bedroom, feeling the humid air of approaching evening brush my face and slightly sway the white cotton curtains of the windows, I realize that she has pulled my most secret part of me into full view without ever discussing it, without ever demanding to know my past history, without ever comparing to anyone or anything. She has done it by freely giving what I most desire, being her seductive self and showing me her most inspiring, sensual side.

I'm a true voyeur. My most exquisite lover with the electric blue eyes has made me face that fact and realize it's a welcomed, natural, necessary trait. How else can a feminine lesbian achieve her true potential?

The first real instance I can recall of possessing this characteristic was as a nine-year-old. My Mom had taken me with her shopping to the Belk-Hudson Department Store in Palatka, Florida. I loved browsing there with Mom. It held the smell of real leather purses, the sights of beautiful earrings and necklaces that graced tabletop stainless steel display cases with mirrored backs and glassed table cases, their bottom shelves covered in artful fashion with crushed velvet in deep burgundies, turquoise greens or champagne beiges.

These big cases held in consummate merchandising magic the very best that the Ladies Department had to offer. Tiny evening bags covered with a million shimmering sequins and mother-of-pearl clasps; exquisite elbow-length evening gloves; wrist-length calfskin driving gloves; white church gloves that had tiny, single pearl and loop closures; and hankies that were singular and unique-linen caressed by Belgian lace or French knots that formed delicate flowers or customized initials.

My Mom always said that a lady of the old Southern tradition possessed two things–a pair of cotton church gloves for the summer months and a signature hanky. Possessing all the required regalia, my Mom was certainly such a lady. I myself was in the gray world of possible ladyship. The gloves were no problem; I had them, but the hanky was another matter. I didn't have one yet. I knew by being sly and observant I would get mine for a Christmas present. Mom worked, considering her task unnoticed, on the tiny, delicately crafted violets that would grace the corners of a beautiful Irish linen square after dinner when she finished chores and picked up her hand-work while watching TV. She hid it in the sewing box under two balls of crochet thread, but, opening the box to "borrow" a thimble (after trading mine to Sylvia Foster for a kiss one Saturday morning on our front porch), I knew the hoped-for possession of social recognition would soon be mine.

I thought about the hanky as I slowly surveyed the display cases. "One never put their hands on the cases." It was a big rule of my Mom. I kept my hands tucked deep in my seersucker pockets. Mom told me it was the best way not to receive glares from the saleslady meaning you were a shopping heathen. I never remembered getting any such glares and I didn't want any. Two of my Mom's friends chatted with her as they browsed the circular rack of dresses about eight feet away. I closed my eyes and took in the ambience, the sophistication, the scents of calfskin mingling with Channel No. 5, the soft whir of the overhead fans, and the softer hum of the fluorescence. This was a gateway to my Mom's world of women, social sophistication, and social acceptance. I loved it!

Never for a moment did I believe this world would represent me when I grew up, but it was a key to what I knew I already admired and wanted to understand–the truly feminine adult woman. I soaked into my pores every scent, touch, sight, and social ritual I could learn from the Ladies Department.

As I admired the display counter that held the

boxed nylon and silk stockings, my Mom continued chatting. The top box of each type of stocking was opened with the top of the box nestled under the bottom. Crispy tissue paper was opened and folded neatly under the box to reveal the stockings. They smelled new and exotic. I particularly held a fondness for the ones that were real silk and had a seam down the back. Learning quickly, I knew from previous experience that if I patiently waited, a serious shopper would approach to survey the merchandise. She would place a beautifully manicured hand into one of the stockings gathered in her opposite hand, cautiously spread her fingers, then slowly, with deliberation, pull her hand from the stocking as she noted its mesh, color, general sturdiness and strength of the hemmed edge that would hold the tags and steel loops of a garter belt.

As I was mesmerized by my fantasy of the stockings being examined by the beautiful lady of my mind, my Mom stunned me into the present with her summons. She had a rack dress over her arm and shooed me with her hand signal toward the row of dressing rooms.

There was a row of four padded, red-burgundy leather, steel-framed chairs that sat outside the dressing rooms. I usually climbed into one of these seats, dangled my feet, and rested my arm on the chilly stainless steel to wait until my Mom was finished trying on clothes. Today she told me to come in with her and hold her purse. I followed her into the spacious stall (by today's standards), pulled the heavy curtain, and climbed onto one of the wooden benches that lined both side walls.

My Mom placed her purse in my lap, hung the rack dress on the hook opposite me, and began to undress.

It was not so much my Mom's undressing that

jolted me into the realization that I loved looking at a woman. It was the finished product and effect when she, attired in the rack dress, stepped back into her high heels, buttoned the last two buttons of the shirtwaist front, turned to face the full-length mirror, straightened her necklace, and smoothed her hair as she gazed into the mirror.

Time *and* my breath sort of stopped for an instant. I was caught spellbound by the woman who gazed at herself in the mirror. Not my Mother, but a beautiful feminine creature stood before me. Tall and thin-boned, she held herself with statuesque composure. I slowly, with delicious intent, observed her from top to bottom—perfectly cut hair, earrings and necklace complimented the dress, a beautifully cut short-sleeved shirtwaist dress of polka-dot taffeta whose full skirt touched her mid-knee in a truly tailored fit. The darts that allowed the bodice to caress her tightly were sewn from waist to bust line. No excessive material. No wasted seam lines. It was a dress and wearer out of a *Life Magazine* fashion ad.

The material was so beautiful, so begging to be admired and touched. The dress bodice was white with tiny, navy blue polka-dots. The skirt, its opposite contrast—blue with white dots. Buttons on the shirtwaist were small-sized solid navy blue. The short sleeves were adorned by even smaller navy blue buttons that pinched close the outer cuffed edges of the sleeves.

Long, graceful legs caressed by nylon stockings led to equally graceful, slim feet nestled in solid blue high heels—the plain, pump style. They oozed perfect coordination and sophistication.

Manicured fingernails displayed the same color as this lovely woman's lipstick (a fifties red that is gaining popularity again, but that will never be duplicated).

This lovely woman in front of me was all that I wanted to discover–vibrant, vital, and in love at the moment with being alive. She was that which I wished to discover, not in myself, but in my first girlfriend. I was hooked. I would search all my life for a woman who would have such beautiful eyes as those that swept the mirror to admire the image reflected there.

The beautiful lady stepped back from the mirror, turned slightly to admire the cut of the dress back and the turn of the heels in the mirror. Over her shoulder she smiled at me.

"Do you like it, Diane? . . . Well, Diane, do you like it? What in the world are you daydreaming about . . . I've asked you three times if you like it? Thinking about another girlfriend?" Johanna's voice drew me from my reverie.

She stood at the end of the bed holding up on a hanger a simply cut, black silk dress that I knew from the length would fall on her mid-knee when she put it on. Her other hand on her hip and steam billowing from the bathroom told me I'd better respond soon. My Johanna loved to linger in the shower and make use of every ounce of hot water the water heater held.

"A perfect choice, Sweetheart. I'll go check the oil in the car before we go."

"Oh, no, Ms. Cole!" she said seductively as she hung the dress on the bedroom door and turned toward the beckoning steam of the next room. "Stay, please. The car's fine. I know you enjoy being observant–history person that you are."

She disappeared into the steam, dropping her jeans

and shirt by the bathroom door.

I'd known J for a while, but not so long as to feel totally comfortable or uninhibited with her dressing in my presence. Some things are, well, personal, but my penchant for what she would do in my presence made me inclined to be eager to stay, to enjoy, to savor. She knew my heart and she demonstrated that evening she would pleasure my visual addiction in a way that no other lover had.

Settling into the chair, resting my feet on the ottoman, I glanced out a window that showed the last sunrays of a spectacular summer evening. Time softened and my busy day melted into the soothing hum of Johanna in the shower. I heard the thud of the bar of soap on the shower floor and a "damn" from her as she fished through the sea of steam to locate it. Resting my head on the back of the chair, I closed my eyes, wished for such happiness to go on forever, and whispered a blessing for Johanna finding me.

I dreamed in earnest of a beautiful lady with Johanna's eyes, shopping for black silk stockings in the Ladies Department of Belk-Hudson as I, a captivated nine-year-old, looked on. The comfort of the chair and my much too busy day combined to allow me to sleep with catnap abandon.

A touch of tender fingers stroking down my cheek woke me. I opened my eyes to Johanna bending close in black low-cut silk and lace bra and black lace bikini panties. She held my chin to the proper inclination with well manicured, polished fingers and gave me a gentle kiss.

"Sleeping through everything, my tired baby? Please, your complete attention as I continue."

"Yes, ma'am," I responded, immediately alert.

Johanna's other hand held her black lace garter belt. The appropriate black seamed silk stockings nestled in one of the old-fashioned thin stocking boxes with folded tissue paper on the bed, its top resting under the bottom to reveal the sensual, erotic, image-provoking contents.

I straightened my position in the chair, placed my arms on the armrests, feet firmly on the floor, and beamed at her. This was my attentive-as-I-can-be position.

She laughed, nodded approval, and turned to position herself between me and the bed.

What she commanded in that fantasy-provoking, erotic-thought-producing display of sensual physical movement and feminine preparedness for stepping with charm and seductiveness into the social dance of cocktails at the Dean's house, always held my heart still with its complete sexual captivation of my senses and its ability to tantalize my erotic imagination. In our time together, she dressed possibly fifteen times for such an event, but, as I would learn with this and future scenarios, this dressing for me in front of me sent my dyke blood streaming through erotic corridors of thought and anticipated activity. It never failed . . . it never lessened . . . it never ceased to captivate my heart and soul. This seductive dance, so well learned, so simple and so full of meaning and innuendo was, in its beauty, comparable to a Japanese tea ceremony.

Facing me, Johanna, with slow deliberation, fastened the garter belt around her beautiful hips, lowering her head to obtain a better view of the adjustment of the garter. Her sensuous, black, shimmering-as-a-raven's-wing hair cascaded across her face and down the front of her shoulders to caress the edges of breasts that bulged just ever so slightly, but ever so seductively from the top of the bra. Her sensual, slender fingers smoothed the belt into final proper placement as she coyly raised her head to stare at me with her best wicked smile. Her eyes held me as she sustained the smile.

My heart pounded. *Concentrate, Diane, concentrate,* I willed myself. *This is no time or situation to begin to sweat. No thought. No racing ahead. Enjoy the situation. All we have are moments. All we have is now.*

She sat upon the bed and gathered up one of the black silk stockings. With practiced precision and the fluidity of graced movement, she raised her leg slightly, bent toward her pointed toe and coaxed the stocking up her leg. Straightening the seam as far as the upper calf, she repeated the sensual procedure on the other leg. Johanna attached the front garter tabs on each leg. Rising from the bed, I thought she would full face me to attach the other garter hooks. Not my unpredictable Johanna. She turned away from me. My unexpected view of her soft back curves, hips that I could caress with my memory, and those long, long legs was more than delightful. It was captivating.

Turning her head toward her left shoulder while pushing back hair falling across her face with her right hand, she whispered so demandingly, "Lover, would you finish the other two. They're just so hard to reach."

Not too hard for me. I could literally reach out from my comfortable viewing position and do the requested. The feel of silk, the tension of the garter tab, and the meshing of both items to create the erotic picture of smooth black silk blending with those long, beautiful legs was enough to make me smile. When I finished both

stockings, I gently cupped the sides of her hips to pull
her closer. Her perfume scented my face as I felt her panties
with my cheek. Heaven should be so exquisite.

"Not now, Diane. We've got time for that later.
Cocktails are at nine. I have to hurry."

Sliding into black three-inch heels which were
waiting by the edge of the bed, Johanna magically
became what I longed for, but not what I longed to be–
the personification of true femininity, true seductiveness
in my mind and also a woman who could gracefully wear
and walk in those beautiful shoes.

She took the few steps to the hook on the bedroom door to retrieve the black dress. Her gait, her
demeanor were so practiced, so easily flowing. I
marveled at her transition from sweater and jean-clad
educator to beautiful seductress. How privileged I was
to see this poetic transformation.

Removing the dress from the hanger, she lowered
the sweetly rustling silk over her body. Johanna wiggled
to let it fall properly and to straighten its lining. Glancing
into the mirror that was almost the length of the door,
she zipped the side closure and adjusted the squared
collarless neck into position. Bought with family money,
a birthday gift from her Mother, the cocktail dress was
simple, superbly cut and formed from expensive material.
Two months of J's salary wouldn't touch the price, but
on her, enhancing all the right curves, flowing freely
sensuous in all the right spots, it was priceless.

Johanna reached to the near dressing table and
adorned her left arm with a wide bracelet of silver then
draped a double loop of long silver chain around her neck.
It was formed of tiny circles each alternating a Celtic knot

and a simple equilateral cross. The chain, so delicate, so eye-catching, draped over her beautiful skin and flowed down upon her exquisite breasts. More than one observer would admire that sensual symmetry of chain and enticing breasts this evening, I imagined, as I observed from my chair.

Again, returning to the mirror, she bent to straighten an errant right leg seam of the black stockings. Smoothing her hands across the silk, she looked pleased at the almost finished product.

Gathering brush and a silver filigreed barrette from the dressing table, she stood in front of the mirror and swept both sides of her hair into one hand held at the back of the top of her head. With brush and barrette still in one hand, she secured the clasp of the barrette and adjusted the tension of her hair in it. Hair, pulled seductively from her high cheekbones, left only tiny, curling wisps at her temples. A begging-to-be-touched bounty of her thick hair fell in two lengths down her back. Even running the brush through it left it seemingly wild and untamed. How I marveled that it looked so different, though she often wore it that way.

Laying down the brush, she picked up lipstick to match the nail polish and applied it while making pouting faces in the mirror.

I could take no more. I rushed from the chair to produce a Kleenex I had grabbed from the box on the bedside table. Advancing from the side, I slowly encircled her waist with my free hand and offered the Kleenex with the other. Her gaze never left the mirror as she retrieved it from my outstretched fingers and concentrated on a perfect blot.

I loved the nearness of her, the scent of her, the

visual stimulation of her that evoked such an urgent need in me. Stepping back one step to admire the finished product, she turned to face me after laying the Kleenex and lipstick on the dressing table. Such loveliness. Such femininity. I never gazed at her enough.

Smiling, she said, "You like it?"

"I do."

"Notice anything different?"

"Oh, yes."

"And that is . . . ?"

She thought I was too enraptured to notice. Wrong, my Johanna. I was concentrating on learning every square centimeter of that sexual, seductive flesh.

"Your makeup. You've found kohl."

"Correct, my professor of admiration and longing glances."

Johanna was never, ever, at a loss to provide the most well-turned phrase at the correct moment.

Those electric blue, see-into-my-heart eyes were precisely outlined in thin, thin bands of stunning black. Only the tiny, sweeping and widening band at the outside of each eye where the thin lines met betrayed their origin. They were exact duplicating lines found on the kohl-adorned eyes of the most famous bust of Nefertiti, but these eye paintings were almost undetectable and unobtrusive. If a truly interested person were to admire her eyes this evening, they would be rewarded with an astounding surprise. The gracefully curving ends of the merging bands held tiny, carefully placed flecks of silver.

"Magnificent. Truly beautiful . . . but how in the Sam Hill did you get the silver in them? It's stunning, coordinated, gorgeous–it's you."

"You napped for several long minutes. I took advantage of my opportunity."

"Ready?" I asked, eager to be out of the house, out into the world to show this beautiful woman off. I knew already that the faculty members, mostly male at this gathering, were about to be held spellbound with beauty they passed unnoticed daily.

"One more thing."

She bent to the dressing table and swirled a bit of patchouli paste from a tiny soapstone jar onto her two fingertips, then onto the pulse points of each wrist. The exotic, sensual, oriental scent wafted through the room. I loved it. I loved her.

Johanna picked up her evening bag covered with a million black shiny sequins and clutched it gracefully in her hand.

"Ready now, Sweetheart."

She looked me up and then slowly down. "You look well–good enough to eat, my wire-rim-spectacled scholar in the dyke apparel." She whistled and pinched my reddening cheek.

J was right. As I swung my arms into my jacket, I contemplated her words. I looked pretty good in my black suit with medium-gray silk shirt that was enhanced by a wide French collar and cuffs that held silver cufflinks. Shiny black, impeccably polished dress oxfords and a silver tie to match J's jewelry rounded out my ensemble. We made a daring and dashing couple. I hoped the faculty was ready for this. My trepidation brought forth enough sweat to curl the wisps of hair at my temples. The rest of my hair was pulled back in a fashion similar to Johanna's. It lacked her feminine style and panache, but it worked okay for a wire-rim adorned scholar.

I eagerly offered my arm, which she accepted. We smiled and made the distance of the hall from the bedroom to the front door with only the spiking taps of J's heels on the hardwood floor breaking our silence as we elegantly sashayed our exit. I was bursting with pride at her loveliness and her allowing me to participate in her most intimate rituals of a transformation into her true self. Conservative suits or sweaters and jeans would never hide Johanna from me again.

Holding the front door open for her, she turned and asked seriously, "Think those liberal-professing academics are ready for this?"

"I hope so. I'm sort of the sticking-out part of this couple."

"You look handsome. Everything will be fine. The Dean told me only two things: be there at nine and my escort should be properly attired in suit and tie. C'mon, Di, no nervous looks. We fit the criteria and I want to go with no one else but you, my Amazon of Academia."

Now I smiled. It was a recent phrase she'd used to describe me, and I loved it. With her speaking those words, I'd have escorted her to hell and back if necessary. Secretly, I hoped the evening would be a little less nerve-racking and demanding than I thought hell would actually be if I had thought it existed at all.

We descended the last two steps to the sidewalk and the waiting car. Johanna laughed confidently and told me that we were going to be truly the most dashing, romantic and adventuresome couple at this stuffy, routine affair. A 'big hit,' she termed it.

I just hoped that I wasn't going to be the one to

get the big hit she was cheerfully describing.

II.

The push that Johanna gave the Dean's doorbell precisely at 9:00 p.m. made a large crack in the conservatism of the institution of higher learning that was her employer. She stood at the door with nerves unruffled, poised, calm. She exuded not only confidence but her non-threatening, non-attention-seeking aura of sexuality. I soaked in her presence, her perfume. Anytime, anywhere–even the Dean's front porch–I never got enough of her.

We could hear the soft music oozing out from the great room that was situated to the left of the house. A lady in her fifties opened the screen door graciously. No locked doors, no formal security in this small Florida town. Not crime nor personal paranoia with whomever might come up the front porch steps was a concern here yet.

"My dear, dear Johanna! It's a pleasure to see you again . . . and your friend is?" Mrs. Dean questioned sincerely while looking me up and down. Her composure did not betray her.

"My escort, Ms. Cole," Johanna explained, "from our neighboring college in Lakeland. Going next term to FSU for advanced studies in intellectual history." She always described my life as more exciting than it actually was. Hugging my arm as she had when we waited for the door to be opened, she beamed at me. I wanted to squirm. I didn't like being the center of attention for however brief a moment.

"Delighted, Ms. Cole. Y'all come on in. I'm sure

Johanna knows everyone here. Please introduce your friend around, dear." Mrs. Dean led us into the room where the music was playing. "I'm sure John will be more than slightly surprised–but delighted, I'm sure–to see you both."

Mrs. Dean then left us and wove her way through a small group of people to find John.

Our entrance into the great room was unnoticed and unspectacular. Most everyone mingled, not in this room, but the huge Florida room that it opened onto. A hundred years ago it would have been the veranda. Today it was converted by half-screen walls and two sets of opened twenty-foot sliding glass doors into the type of room we Southerners craved in the summer–a room filled with wicker made plush with comfortable, floral print pillows; soft humming ceiling fans; and a buffet table at one end that held hors d'oeuvres and a splendid spread of real supper food. No one would go away hungry from the feast spread out this evening.

As we walked about one-fourth of the way through the great room the music stopped. A woman stepped to the stereo system to find more music. The lull in the music let everyone hear the silence that had lain beneath. J had warned me the group was, well, rather stuffy. I guess she was right. A few glasses tinkled with ice. There were a few low, unemotional, uninspired conversations being conducted. It looked like a gathering of my junior high school gym dances. Men stood in several clumped groups near the buffet, while the women made use of the comfortable wicker chairs in two groups at the other end of the veranda space. Miss Scarlet O'Hara would have pouted. There was no, for lack of a better word, social gaiety happening at 9:00 p.m. on this Friday night at the Dean's house.

In my heart of hearts I knew the woman on my arm wouldn't let the situation stay this way. J didn't always need to be the center of attention, but she hated for not every drop of life to be lived to the fullest. This definitely wasn't what she considered the fullest.

Standing still, nearly in the center of the great room, we summed up the situation quickly. I imagined that J was concentrating on how to liven things up. I was concentrating on which group we were supposed to join.

The wicker was calling to me, but I didn't notice any coats or ties in that direction. Maybe we could remain where we were positioned and become the liberal sexual and social fringe of the room that was a median between the split social and heterosexual groups on either end of the room. The thought made me smile.

J released my arm and acknowledged the distinguished gentleman who approached through the much too silent group that was beginning to have its attention riveted upon us. It just wasn't attention I saw and felt. It was stares and whispered asides among themselves and nudged elbows accompanied by nodding heads that returned whispers. This was way, way too much attention for me.

Before the gentleman reached us, Johanna turned to me and whispered through her smile, "Who do you think they're looking at?"

What a question! How silly. "ME!" I exclaimed softly, but emphatically, in capital letters.

"You might be right, Sweetheart, but I was hoping you'd say me. Don't you think I'm just about killer gorgeous this evening?"

My fears lessened. "Sure. It's you. Who of either sex couldn't but admire those gorgeous legs of yours."

J was always that way. Even if I was in the eye of the storm, she would lessen my anxiety with a bit of practical humor. It worked a smidge, and I took my first good deep breath in minutes.

The distinguished gentleman stood front and center and presented two drinks. To Johanna he offered a beautifully cut crystal goblet filled with red wine. To me a scotch on the rocks in a more practical, solid, unadorned selection of glassware.

"Johanna, my dear, so lovely to see you." He looked Johanna over with admiring eyes. "You're simply elegant this evening . . . and you, Ms. Cole, are a privileged escort." He said this while staring at me with steady eyes that twinkled. "I've learned, Ms. Cole, that Johanna will push the envelope of any situation. Not very practical for the conservatism of an academic life in the truly traditional South, but while she still has a career, I hope she never stops."

He looked at Johanna, who sipped the wine slowly while those long, beautifully manicured, seductive fingers cradled and enhanced the stunning crystal cuts that glistened in the overhead light. Holding a long look at Johanna, he truly admired what he saw.

I knew right then and there I liked Mr. Dean. He was a connoisseur of the truly beautiful, the truly daring, the truly unpredictable that a life well-lived would hold.

As he assumed a more casual stance by sliding one hand into his trouser pocket, Mr. Dean questioned me, "Hope you don't mind the scotch? Beverly (Mrs.

Dean) said 'escort' and well, all the other males are drinking it."

"It's absolutely superb, sir," I commented after my first sip. It was top quality and something that my increasing uneasiness had subconsciously sought. How could Mr. Dean know that the first taste of a truly good scotch (usually a much larger gulp than what I consumed in his presence) with its feel searing my throat as I drank it and the heat, the fire, the settling that it would pulse through my blood was something that I was partaking of more and more? He couldn't. I silently gave thanks for his fateful choice, for giving me what I craved. All I said as my mind prepared for the effect of the glass I held was, "It's my drink of choice and most welcomed at this moment."

"I'm glad, dear. Didn't want to get the evening off to a bad start. Please, enjoy the food and the company. Make yourself at home. Anything you need, just ask. Life should be enjoyed, don't you believe, in all its myriad forms, as they say. Have a great evening."

Mr. Dean acknowledged Johanna again, and as he turned to go, the stereo started up. I gazed beyond his shoulder, as that instant slowed in time, to see the gender-split groups giving their complete attention to Mr. Dean interacting with us. Maybe this evening was only going to be stares and whispers. Lesbians out of the closet and out of place. I hoped not. I wanted to enjoy Johanna in her surroundings with her colleagues. Sometimes something as little as a tie or black dress oxfords can be a stumbling block to true interaction. Why do we see so superficially? Why do we sometimes have to be more than ourselves just to be ourselves?

Within the instant of my observation, Mr. Dean held

out his hand to J and asked if she would enjoy dancing
to Glen Miller.

She took his hand but leaned to me and whispered,
"Diane, the last dance is yours, always yours."

Mr. Dean interjected by coming nearer us. "Do
you mind terribly, Ms. Cole? This lady is just too beautiful
not to accompany on the dance floor. It'll remind me of
my youth."

"No problem. Enjoy."

Johanna handed me the wine glass. They both
smiled and, as Mr. Dean escorted her to the center of the
veranda, they slid into the sensual stream of Glen Miller
as it softly permeated the two rooms.

With the first six bars they danced, J only grew
more lovely, more alluring, and Mr. Dean became, again,
the cavalier gentleman of his youth. The room took on
their ambiance, their aura of life. Chatter and eyes were
placed on them. Most of the folks in the room were older
and Mr. Miller brought back hidden smiles and laughter.

Miss Scarlet O'Hara would have felt better about '
this situation. There was beginning to be some life in this
party. A few men walked to the wicker chairs and sought
out dance partners. Laughter and music, the general hum
of pleasant talk by people familiar with each other, mingled
together in the stream of sensuality that floated around
us. I left our glasses on a table by a wicker chair and
moseyed to the buffet for some supper. Hors d'oeuvres
were for required, stuffy, social functions. Supper was in
order. This was beginning to be a pretty great party.

I occupied a chair in a group of four plus a small
settee clustered around a glass coffee table on the one
corner of the veranda. Two end tables with antique table

lamps completed the setting. It was a cozy nook that the
three women who acknowledged my joining them with
nods and smiles had probably lounged in many, many
times. While I leisurely munched and finished my drink,
they chatted about children, church social functions and
the Whetston's bar-b-que that everyone had attended last
Saturday. They all agreed that Carol Whetston made the
best potato salad in town.

Listening to their familiar conversation was not my
main interest. My view was unhindered to the veranda-
turned-dance-floor. The '40s music continued and more
couples danced. Johanna would catch my eye on a turn
or over her partner's shoulder and give me a wink and
smile. I returned them. After surveying the veranda after
several songs were completed, I realized that the group
of males standing near the buffet were actually a dance
queue for Johanna. After each song, she'd approach the
group where some smiled and chatted with her in
animated fashion. Their control of the situation was belied
by the fact that some stuffed their hands in their pockets
like nervous ten-year-olds. She was asking them to
dance, not vice versa.

Wondering how the ladies not dancing were
taking this, I nonchalantly observed the "wicker" as I
finished my second scotch. A few were absorbed in seemingly serious conversation, but most sat with arms folded
and glared toward the buffet table as they chatted.
Neither J nor her escort was making any friends on this
end of the room.

The chairs near me were vacated by a few women.
More women congregated in the kitchen, and I hoped
they were tending a coffeepot I had searched in vain to

locate at the buffet. It's a very old rule–women gather at the hearth of a home.

I lounged comfortably and with my crossed leg kept time to the swing band music with my foot. Contemplating whether to mingle or sit, I sat. There was time, lots of time, in the evening to mingle.

A woman attired in an expensive pantsuit sauntered by, just out of the kitchen, holding a coffee cup. She slowed near me and smiled. "Mind if I join you? The kitchen's getting a little crowded."

"Sure, please. I'd enjoy the company."

She set the cup and saucer on the table with my empty glass and sat gracefully in the chair next to me. "I saw you come in. Are you a . . . eh, friend of Johanna's?" Her brown eyes were so intense, so expressive. They questioned so much more than her simple sentences.

"Diane, my name is Diane Cole."

"Pleased. I'm Mary Beth Williams. My husband is third from the right at the buffet table. He's a colleague of Johanna's. Got tenure two years ago."

I looked across the veranda and located him easily.

"Richard says Johanna is gay."

Well, Mary Beth Williams was certainly direct. No minced words. No beating around the bush. "I believe she prefers being described as lesbian." I continued to observe her husband as I spoke.

"I see," she continued. "I was under the impression that lesbians look like you."

Still direct. Still no minced words.

"How do I look, if you don't mind my asking?" Miss Scarlet O'Hara would have appreciated my manners under this extreme, blunt scrutiny.

"Like a sinful, depraved, sexually perverse dyke."
The words were spoken with a venomous overtake, but
with a cool, practiced exterior. She retrieved her cup and
saucer as I switched my gaze toward her.

Now the sweat started in earnest, but it would not
break my concentration on Mrs. Williams. The muscles
in my gut and back tightened. I wished the glass on the
end table contained more liquid. Such hate disguised by
such beauty.

She did not get up or continue to speak. Her glare
and vicious smile held me like a cornered bit of prey. A
comeback. Something shocking. Something mean. Think
. . . No need to fight the vicious with the vicious. It wasn't
my nature.

"I see, Mrs. Williams. I thought you were going to
compliment my suit. Johanna picked it out. She says it
makes me look rather dashing, rather handsome. She told
me that any woman with any bit of sense wouldn't pass
up the opportunity to go to bed with a woman who looks
as good as I do in a suit." The scotch was definitely doing
its job. I never was so verbal, so talkative with someone
I didn't know. Now I smiled with my often hidden to the
world Amazon confidence and reached for the empty
glass.

Mrs. Dean approached my chair and firmly
patted my shoulder. "I'll get that, Ms. Cole. You look
like something to drink is exactly what you need. Mary
Beth, isn't Richard motioning for you to join him?"

Mary Beth glared at Mrs. Dean, placed the cup
and saucer on the table, and barged her way toward
Richard through the dancing couples.

I got up with the empty glass in hand and turned

toward Mrs. Dean, "I could use another, thanks." I realized that all our preparation for life's situations often leaves us unprepared. My big hit of the evening did not come from a manly right hook but from a beautiful woman's hateful words.

"She's such a bitch, Ms. Cole. Please overlook her brutish narrowness. I've been in the kitchen trying to dissuade her from such a confrontation. Believe me, she's envious of you with Johanna. She deplores seeing anyone happy. The both of you exude it. It's beyond her capacity to endure. Let's talk of something else. Would you like to tour the house?"

"Yes. A diversion would be greatly appreciated."

Mrs. Dean and I slowly toured every room of the 1860s home. It was comfortable but surprisingly spacious, for such a dated house. The abundance of closets, which were huge, were accomplished by converting small bedrooms to a newer purpose. Even the bathrooms were to be admired. Mrs. Dean had done all the wallpapering and refinishing of the hardwood floors. The house held Mr. Dean's inherited antiques, and it held Mrs. Dean's heart. What time, patience, and love she had contributed to make this house a home. Even crocheted doilies and embroidered scarves and tablecloths graced all the appropriate spots.

Finishing up the tour, we made the last descending steps of the staircase and faced the veranda. Johanna and most of the men had mingled to the women's wicker section and taken up positions. Mr. Dean was providing a seated Johanna with a plate of delectables from the buffet and Mary Beth's husband was procuring another glass of wine for her. The room was filled with music and laughter, but predominantly with an electrical, static-inducing kind of sexual energy that had everyone's aura slightly a-tingle. Mrs. Dean held my elbow gently and guided me toward the situation. I noticed J's long, beautiful legs, with those wicked, wicked stockings and heels, had more than a few of the male conversationalists enticed. She looked so beautiful and naturally unaware that she was about the most stunning creature in the room.

Mrs. Dean introduced me to all the men sitting and standing around J. I got firm, overconfident handshakes and nods of recognition. Richard Williams said he spoke for all his colleagues when he said I'd escorted the most beautiful woman of all to the party. Nods and comments of agreement were warmly appreciated by me, but they did not assuage the glare I received from Mary Beth.

Johanna munched with the practiced sophistication of being able to balance plate and napkin gracefully while I told the group "a little about myself" as she urged me to do. I talked about growing up the daughter of a fisherman instead of the academic life I now led. How could I compete with their lives of tenure and publishing? It worked. I hooked them with my most harrowing experiences on the river and my ability, not to fly-fish, but to cast net and trout line. Let's just say I got a little carried away and consumed all the time until Johanna finished her supper. The gentlemen were rapt with attention and respect. What I knew and talked about was man's work, and they admired that. Even a few of the seated women listened attentively.

Finishing up the story about setting one thousand hooks at 4:00 a.m. during the Northeaster of the previous Thanksgiving, I ended my gaze of the group on Johanna.

She reclined relaxed, but poised. Her hand rested on Mr. Dean's hand that lay on the same chair arm as hers while he occupied an ottoman beside her chair. She saw me look at her hand, but she only smiled contentedly at me. She made no attempt to remove hers from his until my story was complete and dancing and varied conversations filled the room again.

I excused myself from the remaining group to follow Mrs. Dean to the kitchen for coffee. Before going, I offered to take J's finished dishes. Handing them to me, she rose from the chair.

"Are you okay, Di? Having a good time? Aren't John and Beverly just adorable?"

"They are and I am," I replied light-heartedly. The guardedness that tinged my voice was sensed by J.

"I'll explain. Don't be upset. Later–when we dance."

Mr. Dean again asked Johanna for a dance and they were off to the other side of the room.

I watched them go and thought maybe her wildness, her hidden side, her ability to totally seduce–and also to control if she wanted–could only be appreciated sufficiently, lived through successfully by someone older. Maybe someone male.

As I headed for the kitchen with Mrs. Dean chatting casually as she led the way, I wished I was heading for a glass of scotch. Why did what I most love about Johanna– her vitality, her intelligence, her sexuality–fill me at times with the dread of an unknown demon that would rise up so unexpectedly?

I knew how Mr. Rhett Butler could have a love-hate relationship with Miss O'Hara.

Mrs. Dean, a few other ladies, and I spent most of the remainder of the evening sitting around the kitchen table swapping stories. Placing my suit jacket on my chair back and loosening my tie to get comfortable, I told them they could just re-interpret some of my stories with a male pronoun, if they wished, and I would fit right in as one of the girls. They eagerly agreed (though a majority felt it wasn't necessary, and the talk fest was on).

Mrs. Lowell spoke of riding a motorcycle in 1927 with her first great love from Englewood Cliffs, New Jersey, to Tampa, Florida. I liked Mrs. Lowell. She had several great loves in her life before settling down to become a college professor's wife.

Mrs. Dean recounted her courtship in a small farming town with Mr. Dean.

Mrs. Rosecrans told of her life in the Ziegfeld Follies. She was still a looker. Age had not diminished her wit, her hell-raising abilities, or her passion for weekly poker games with the other "girls" who sat around the table. She made me promise not to divulge one of their most hidden poker secrets. I promised and was rewarded with the fact that they partook of Mr. Dean's best scotch and cigars during their games. They all howled, laughed unstoppably, and wiped tears from their eyes when Mrs. Rosecrans spilled the secret. These women whom years had given happiness and hardship, were devilish thirteen-year-olds at heart.

Mrs. Jacobs spoke of adopting two sons and working in an airplane factory during World War II. The pictures she produced of her sons showed two handsome adults. One was a lawyer, one a researcher in the pharmaceutical industry.

Mrs. Evans related surviving cancer and having a son killed in Korea. Her passion was collecting photographs that were of the Civil War era.

Mrs. Barnhill was a fifth generation Floridian. Her family held 42,000 acres of prime citrus that was now a part of the central Florida co-op of growers. She financed her husband's love of expensive fishing boats.

Mrs. Smith had trained as a nurse but loved the outdoors more. She met her husband while working for the park service, and he was on summer vacation which he used every year to explore the Rockies. Now they explored in a Winnebago with two grandchildren on their summer expeditions.

I told, at Mrs. Dean's request, how I had met Johanna. Giving a generally sparse outline, they wanted more–the juicy details.

Was Johanna a Femme? Was I a Butch?

What was it like to kiss a woman?

Had I ever been to a lesbian bar?

Was it like those in the porno movies?

Had I ever slept with a man?

What was it like to be "in love" with a woman?

Did I wear boxers?

Did a woman lover understand you better than a man?

Mrs. Rosecrans, who admitted to a little "girlie fling" while in the Follies, compared notes. The woman knew what she was talking about and how to get the response desired from the girlie under topic. I decided she had had much more than a fling. Much, much more.

Her friends were delighted with her information, though they wondered why in the hell she hadn't divulged it long ago.

I believe Miss Scarlet O'Hara would have considered our girl talk to be most productive, most risqué, and slightly bordering on the scandalous for the conservative college town the group at the table was supposed to represent.

As we chatted and sipped the best Columbian coffee I've ever tasted, I surveyed the women at the table. True friends for longer than I'd been alive. True friends in good and bad. True friends who honestly admitted the heart bonds at this table were stronger than with their husbands. Mrs. Dean wiped tears with a paper napkin and looked at me. I saw someone my Mother's age, but someone who, for a moment–letting just a glint of sadness show in her eyes–I felt somehow had more in common with me.

J interrupted our chatter and giggles. "It's time, Ladies of the Kitchen, for the last dance. C'mon and give these gents a surprise. Show them that y'all can really still cut a rug."

More howls from the table. Mrs. Rosecrans suggested that she and Russell would probably just tap their canes to the music, since they both had hip replacements. The poker band of merry women agreed that would be just fine. Everyone hurried from the kitchen to find their partners before the music could start.

Allowing the poker band out first, I was last to leave the kitchen. When I reached the doorway, J seductively led me by the tie to the veranda. She smiled and admired. She winked her baby blues and batted sexily those long eyelashes that were really hers. I loved her. How could I stay mad or worried? With the music beginning,

I took her in my arms and laid my head on her shoulder. She caressed my hair and kissed me on the cheek. The sway, the feel of her, the scent of her passion-heightening perfume persuaded me to close my eyes–to just drift, to just be in her arms.

She whispered, "The kohl was such a hit. Even the women asked about it."

I nestled closer to her.

"Did you really have a good time, baby? John says we should come and visit without a formal party involved."

"I'd love to. How 'bout a kiss from the most gorgeous woman in the room?"

J gave me one of her most gentle, most seductive kisses, then asked, "Like the music? I picked it out just for you. I know it's your favorite." She traced my back and shoulders with her strong, capable fingers.

I didn't care who noticed. I didn't care who whispered. Johanna was in my arms and the stereo played Mr. Cole Porter's, "Anything Goes." Not the fast Frank Sinatra-like version, but a slow-tempered '40s style that held long, long moments of non-lyrical rifts of jazz piano. It was beautiful. She was beautiful.

J stopped moving to the music. I opened my eyes to find Mrs. Dean holding J's shoulder. Turning to her, Johanna smiled. "I'm sure Diane would love to dance. I'll just find John to finish the music with."

"He's waiting right over there," Mrs. Dean spoke and moved her eyes toward her husband at the edge of the dance floor. He stood tall, poised. The true cavalier waiting for a beauty to join him Johanna sashshayed gracefully through the crowd. I stared at Mrs. Dean.

This wasn't Saturday night at a lesbian bar in

Orlando. Taking Mrs. Dean in my arms could mean trouble for me–but much worse trouble for her–and possible disaster for Johanna.

There's something about a determined woman that will not be denied. Sensing my hesitation, my quandary, Mrs. Dean said confidently, while taking me in her arms, "I'll lead and speak. Please, just listen."

I thought my most horrid visions were now about to be realized. She was going to tell me J was having an affair with her husband.

We danced cheek to cheek. I was glad Mrs. Dean couldn't see the tears in my eyes. Even in that gut-wrenching, send-my-heart-to-hell moment, I noticed the little things. She was a great dancer. J always said my attention to detail got me off the big picture, away from hurt and sorrow. This time I hoped she was right.

"Guess you never expected your evening to end like this, Diane . . . may I call you that?"

"Yes, you can . . . well . . . no, I wasn't quite expecting this."

"It doesn't matter what the people in this room think, do, or say about this, er, you know, situation I've now put you in. John has enough professional clout to take care of anything. I must tell you a few things–why J is so the way she is around John.

"Please." I danced and prayed for the next terrible words not to be actually spoken.

"Where to begin in a few words. John and I are both so taken with Johanna. We know why our daughter, Elizabeth, was so in love with her. Not just a high school crush. True love found at an early age. A blessing. That leaves all the time in the world for happiness."

The tears fell fast from my eyes and slid down my cheeks, dampening Mrs. Dean's beautiful dress, as her tears were now wetting my silk shirt.

"Yes, ma'am."

"Has J told you about Elizabeth?"

"No, ma'am."

"Well, I'll finish what I've begun. They were so happy in high school. So . . . meant to be together. Our daughter went her summer after graduation to New York's Greenwich Village, 'to find herself.' J had family obligations and was going to join her at New York University in the fall."

"Yes, ma'am."

"That terrible summer Elizabeth died of an overdose and J fell apart. Our families are close. She became more to us than Elizabeth's lover. She became a living legacy of what Elizabeth should have experienced. She became our own. We took her under our wing and never let go. Is that so terrible?"

"No, ma'am."

"J told us all about you. You are as gentle and witty as she described, but she never told us about how in love with her you are."

"Yes, ma'am. I am."

The final jazz rift ended and everyone applauded and began good-byes for home.

Mr. Dean approached his wife with pocket handkerchief in hand. "I'll see to the folks leaving. Don't worry about them." He kissed her on the cheek.

J approached me, pulling my pocket handkerchief from the inside breast pocket of my jacket. "You look like you could use this. Are you okay? I'll explain everything."

"No need to, J," I replied between wiping tears and blowing my nose. "No need to say anything–ever. I love you as you are."

I did, and I still do.

I knew the closeness the couple held to Johanna and how I'd read the signals all wrong. It taught me a valuable lesson. Only let what you observe speak for itself. No one I'd ever met tended Johanna with this much closeness, this much concern, this much love. They even called her J. Only those that touched her heart did that.

We made our last good-byes and hugs on the front porch. I stood there now, not with the trepidation I'd brought, but with sadness that life had dealt them all such a cruel hand. I stood there also with eagerness and purpose. Purpose to abide with the wild, unspoken sadness that sometimes overtook Johanna. Eagerness to become more familiar with this couple around whom she was so herself.

The last hug was Mrs. Dean to me as I held Johanna's hand.

"You'll come back soon. I want to get to know you much better. You have the heart J needs. Not one, I'm afraid, Elizabeth could truly offer. She was as wild, as possessed of life as Johanna."

"We'll be back. Two weeks from Sunday to take you up on that dinner invitation," I assured them both.

With the stars out and the moon setting over the bay, I escorted my lady to the car and helped her in. J said nothing from porch to car. A long gap for someone so inclined to talk. A short time for one like me so inclined to silence. As I walked from passenger to driver's side, I thought about the hurt, the sadness, the loneliness they all possessed. I felt their interaction held more–the possibility of life and the possibility of a not so sad future. I was hoping to find a blessing in this sad state of affairs. Hoping that as Mr. Cole Porter wrote, "Heaven Knows, Anything Goes." Hoping that that "anything" would contain happiness for us all.

I'm sure Miss Scarlet O'Hara would have considered it a wonderful party filled with intensity, drama, innuendo, suspense, sexual allure and lots of wonderful chitchat. Though I was very happy to be leaving with the most stunning and intriguing guest there, I felt the loss, the devastation of life and its possibilities, and the great sadness that encompassed it all. It felt to me as if the situation mirrored the gut-wrenching heartbreak felt at the burning of Atlanta.

III.

It had been quite a party. Full of whispers, intrigue, suspense and lots of emotion. As I traveled through the summer night of central Florida listening to the AM station, I drove on nearly deserted streets with my mind not entirely on the road. Carley Simon sang on the radio– one of my favorites, "Anticipation." I whispered the words, thinking of the most beautiful woman at the party. She occupied my front passenger seat, asleep with her head reclined on the seat back.

The last stoplight on the edge of this small, small town caught us. I stopped, respectful of the law. I could have run it easily. Light from the last two streetlamps in town illuminated my third-hand car.

Johanna, she with the most exquisite blue eyes,

she of such wild temperament and stubborn determination, she who held my dyke heart with her seductive body, sensual presence, intriguing intelligence, turned to me, head still resting on the seat.

"You could have run the light. Always predictable. *So* a follower of the rules. Don't you want to live just a little bit, my academic Amazon?"

With that softly whispered inquiry, Johanna let her intentions be known as she placed her '50s . . . red manicured fingers lightly on my trousered leg and tapped softly, impatiently, for my response.

I could no longer hold my pretended concentration on the light's importance. Gazing at her, my heart pounded, and I had to smile in anticipation. Still, after hours of dancing and sashaying among the obligatory guests of the Dean's cocktail party, she was stunning. Even in the relaxed pose of being chauffeured by the luckiest person in the universe, she was simply gorgeous in her unpretentious beauty.

I took her in, as I loved to do. The strong line of her chin and jawbone was model perfect. I never lost the desire, or opinion, that that beautiful jaw was always begging to be kissed. Her lips were luscious with color that matched her nails. Her smile could captivate, cajole or criticize in an instant. It was so without sham or insincerity that it unknowingly drew you in. That ready smile helped Johanna never meet a stranger.

She still looked fresh in the expensive black silk dress. Her long silver chain was perfectly roped around her neck twice, gracing her collarbone with refinement and following the curve of her sensual breasts. Dangling as seductively on this beautiful femme as a beckoning finger of her hand would motion me to follow her to bed, it held my attention. I thought about the metaphorical possibilities of being beckoned to her bed.

Her long, long legs in seamed black stockings gracefully crossed as the dress fell just about two left-to-your-imagination inches above her knee. Her feet were comfortable in stiletto heels. How she danced in them was beyond my comprehension. It was an ability that intrigued my dyke curiosity and accounted for my daydreams while doing research in the library. Her slender should-be-kissed feet in those stockings and heels made me have a definite itch for research–but not the academic kind.

I was thankful for the Fates placing me under the streetlamps with time to study and admire J, my beautiful Hungarian gypsy. That she had found me (a story in itself), that she had pursued me, was a wonderment. I considered her professionally and sexually out of my league, but I hoped–in my heart of hearts–she would put up with a slightly unschooled, gangly dyke who possessed more natural inclination than experience. She said often to me that she saw great potential that only needed nurture and guidance. In my "potential," I hope she included perfected sexual pleasuring and the ability to drive her wild. I prayed that it was not only in the area of academic publishing.

Her black sequined evening bag with pearl clasps glinted a thousand prism lights reflected by the streetlamps. Johanna cradled it in her lap with her right hand. The tapping on my leg had transformed itself into J's hand sensually massaging my upper leg. I imagined how it would have felt without the trouser material as a barrier.

The glow in the car turned from red-tinged to

green. It only gave me a different ambience to study her. My eyes continued to drink her in.

She smiled, as her hand continued to tempt my concentration.

"Well," she whispered enticingly, "don't you want to live–just a little?"

"Sure," was all I managed to respond.

Our friends marveled, even in our brief time together, that the never-at-a-loss-for-words Johanna could possibly date someone so . . . well . . . quite bluntly, shy and untalkative. I can tell you that honestly. Always, I've had the knack of plainly seeing my worst faults.

Johanna stared unseeingly at the stoplight as I looked at her. "Diane, I'm real sorry about this evening. I should have told you about John. That's a big mistake." She bit her lip and continued to stare straight ahead. "It's just, well, so complicated. I'm afraid if you knew, it might make you feel so . . . so . . . encumbered with a lot of my personal baggage. That's the major reason I didn't tell you." J stared ahead, beyond the stoplight into a future that should have held different possibilities.

"The minor would be?"

"Always the wit, eh, Ms. Cole?" She turned to me again, with tears in her eyes. "I thought this time would be different, that I wouldn't be so attracted, so comfortable, with the situation. "No . . ." Silence is often the greatest generator of truth. ". . . I don't want to lose you," she continued. "I want you to see only the side of me that will hold you."

It had been quite an evening, and I now gazed at J with tears in my eyes. She didn't want to lose me! What irony! My sentence structure got a little more complex as

I put my heart into my words. "You'll never lose me until you feel that it's necessary. My dearest Johanna, I'm in love with you. Just let me see all of you, no matter what. Agreed?"

"Agreed," she managed to respond with a not so sad voice. Wiping tears from her cheeks, she nodded and continued to stare straight ahead.

My heart felt the possibility, the strength, and the adventure of those uttered words. I'd never said them to anyone before.

"There's just one thing, Diane . . . ."

"Yes?"

"Perhaps we could move toward my house? We've sat through two cycles of the stoplight. Thank God this town is so small. No rear-ending possibilities."

I revved the engine. We were off. Neil Diamond crackled on the AM.

J moved close to me. Her hand continued to rest reassuringly on my leg. "One day, I hope you get more than just one station."

One day I would. One day I'd have the top of the line sedan with Dolby Surround that would truly compliment J's natural elegance. Tonight we headed toward her house with rolled-down windows that enfolded us with hot, clinging humidity. The weather matched my anticipation. I wanted to be the hot, clinging dampness that would enfold Johanna.

As we stood on J's porch with light-bugs swarming around the light, a deep clap of thunder from across the bay rattled the windows by the door. I rattled the keys, trying to suavely open the door for J to enter. J held my free arm and waited patiently. I jiggled the key in the lock, not sure if my consumption of scotch at the party or J's nearness was playing havoc with my concentration. Johanna, in her heels, dominated my surroundings and my senses with her exquisite perfume. I concluded she was my major lack of concentration.

"Let me help."

I admitted defeat, "Okay, you try."

"No problem," she laughed. J calmly took one step toward the door and placed a forceful, flat-footed kick mid-length of the bottom half. The door opened obediently. "It always sticks."

I was impressed. Strong, full of concentration, truly professional; in those heels it compared to the best kicking style in the NFL. She encircled my shoulder with her arm to escort me inside. I loved J but knew my time of dyke reckoning had come. What if she wasn't so pleased when my bed talents didn't compare to my verbal acclamation? I hesitated slightly. She sensed my movement and stopped beside me. I swallowed hard and looked to the floor. She looked at the floor as if we'd both discovered something important there. I was thankful for her gesture. Her piercing gaze couldn't have been sustained by me at this moment.

"Scared? Never done this before?"

"No–I mean yes." I gathered my composure. "No, not scared. Yes, I've done it before."

"Afraid you might not be as skilled, let us say, as you think I'm used to? Afraid that your ineptitude might cloud my judgment of your abilities?"

J always could read my heart even though I could hide it so easily from others. She, with the sometimes deeper than indigo eyes, would make me be myself always–regardless of the consequences, regardless of the assumptions I would be required to abandon. She was blunt, but she was right.

"Yes," I agreed and suddenly decided I didn't want to proceed farther into the house.

She held her stance. "Do you consider yourself a butch?"

"Yes."

"You think that should compliment my femme self?"

"Yes," I agreed.

She kissed my cheek. "I concur. We'll be fine. It takes a strong dyke to admit performance anxiety. You might be surprised that we'll learn a lot about each other. Things you can't imagine at this moment. You're a true dyke, Diane, and I love you for that, but I also love you for so much more."

She said she loved me! I had guts and inspiration to move to the bedroom even if it was half a world away. The sweat of trepidation that soaked my shirt was now bearable on my skin. I hoped that soon the sweat of Johanna would replace it.

J led me by my loosened tie to the bedroom door and stopped. Turning to me, both of us wedged in the bungalow's small, seventy-year-old doorframe. I could feel the curves, the softness, and the temptation that I so desperately wanted to consume. The circumstance made me hot, but J was poised and cool. How, was beyond my comprehension.

"Just have a seat in that big ol' chair, Sweetheart. I'll be back." She tapped through the house, shutting tall sash windows against the rain. I sat in the overstuffed chair by her bed and waited . . . waited for the sound of her heels to return. Faintly approaching, their pulse matched my heartbeat. With their increased strength, my blood surged, and the throbbing began to dampen me and the chair. I could tell she was a practitioner who knew how to build for effect.

Seeing her in the doorway, I instinctively rose, ready to be suave, slightly charming, and oh, so predatory. She held her hand for me to halt and walked into the bathroom that was on the opposite wall from me. I sat, not feeling rejected but slightly off cue. Minutes passed as I conjured more fantasies, mentally rehearsed more moves.

Returning fully clothed, she lounged against the bedroom door. "No need to ruin that beautiful silk shirt with all that makeup, eh, Diane?"

She struck a model's relaxed pose on the doorframe. That had to be my cue. I started to rise, way more than ready, revved and gunning.

Her hand halted me. I'd definitely no butch control of this unfolding foreplay. My face showed my concern, my willingness to be on with the chase.

She smiled her wicked, wicked smile. Backlit by the bathroom light and revealed by lightning flashes that edged closer, Johanna struck a picture of sensuality and control. Her piercing eyes stared me down into submission.

"Ms. Cole, before we begin," (the 'Ms.' drawn out in the longest, sexiest syllable I'd ever imagined), "I'm going to do something I don't believe anyone's ever done to you, or for you." She held her pose, gently rubbing a forefinger in small circular motions on her silky thigh.

I breathed hard but silently. Be cool. Be confident. "That would be?" I almost whispered, trying to sound rather experienced.

"I'm going to feed that visual addiction I know you possess."

I swallowed several times. No one knew of my most secret of passions. I gripped the armrests and contemplated the words. My older dyke friends wouldn't admit to the inclination though the phrase, "real good look" turned up in their conversations. I'd chained that need against the wall of conventionality. In my previously small circle of lovers, I never thought I would feel satisfaction of that desire.

Sweating in anticipation, I tensed in the chair. My most prized possibility stood before me, but I didn't quite know the rules of procedure.

J stepped from the door in a slow, slow heart-breaking, sensual model's walk where angular form was accompanied by a sensual aura that smoothed her into beautiful curves. Smiling, she took the six-foot runway walk that would place her directly in front of me.

Laughingly, she directed, "Just relax. Put your feet on the ottoman. You've waited a long time." She then seriously added, "Engage your true self." As she advanced in her sensual stalking, "Oh, yes, enjoy. I almost forgot the best part."

Still seductively smiling, still in photographic perfection, Johanna began a sexual mandala–a vision of exquisite, sense-heightening art for me. I've satisfied the need in ensuing years, but no one's ever done it with such grace, natural style, or passion.

Her hand, with those delicate, strong fingers, flowed from her side to her ribcage to her breasts, where she rubbed the black silk. She massaged and teased her nipples until they were taut even through the layers.

Caressing her collarbone, then neck, she ran those gliding hands farther until her spread fingers played through the long wild hair behind her ears. Those hands felt the dampness hidden at the back of her neck. Swimming in the sensual ocean and soft skin her fingers discovered, she threw her head back slightly and closed her eyes. She became concentrated, lost in her own pleasure, and at that instant I became a true voyeur in observing the scene of this woman's self-gratification.

Details heightened, time displaced into a sexual slowness, the room warmed and I settled. My heart pounded with every touch she made on her gorgeous ivory skin. My sexual desires grew, not with anticipation, but with the superb grace and beauty of each moment.

Hipbones swayed ever so slightly as she widened her stance. Hands mingled in that silky dark hair that the heat of our situation now curled in wispy ringlets around her face. Finding the filigreed barrette, she unbound her hair, shook her head, and let her true self begin to emerge. She combed her fingers through the cascading hair. My wild Hungarian gypsy appeared as she leveled a gaze into my heart with those blue eyes. Her smile closed, held a long moment, then her tongue, slowly, oh so slowly, wet her lips.

I instinctively returned sexual approval by wetting mine.

Lightning flashed closer as J held my gaze and undid the side zipper on the black dress. I observed her jewelry was missing. She required none in her emerging natural state.

She bent slowly, slightly from the waist and grasped the hem and began to pull, to peel conventionality farther from herself, to expose to me what she truly was. Up it came, revealing the tops of black-seamed stockings and black lace garter belt. The curves of her outer thighs caught the storm flash and wisps of black hair crept from the black silk, low cut panty. A perfect fit. They kissed her hips and swung under her navel across a muscular stomach—muscles that begged to be touched. My fingertips imagined the softness of her skin, the texture of the fine, curling escaping black hairs that I wanted to nestle again into their proper home of the silk panty.

The dress moved slowly higher. Torso and ribcage appeared. Not as calm as I supposed. Droplets of sweat inched down her, glistening like stars of the Milky Way in very close lightning flashes. I wished I could read that star chart with my feel of her skin, to lap up that Milky Way with my tongue, to place constellations of kisses upon the ever-more-revealing sky of her body.

Higher still, the dress unveiled her breasts that were encased in the black silk and lace bra. They were generous, enticing, and as seductively displayed as the rest of J. Their fullness bulged ever so slightly from the top of the bra. Just enough to create the cleavage the silver necklace had accentuated. Just enough to be alluring. Just enough to captivate my desire to see more.

One final tug and J shook her head from the dress, truly setting her hair to primitive abandon. She winked as she laid it, with care, over the straight-back chair at arm's length.

I nodded for her to continue. She spoke the only words of her erotic pleasuring. "Like what you see, Diane? Want to see more?"

I nodded again, and the dance of beauty my eyes

desired continued.

She posed in front of me in every seductive stance I'd ever imagined. The flashes of lightning became the flashbulbs that my mind focused upon her to capture her visual pictures I will never forget. Losing herself in her own pleasuring, her own discovery, she traced fingers through ever curve she possessed, felt muscles and desire with embracing hands, and swayed and moved in those heels with grace and a flow of sensuality many will not give up self-control to experience.

My heart beat to her ever-wilding abandon. Ecstasy could possibly hold greater pleasures, but I would never search its horizons for them.

The paned windows of the bedroom shook as a true Florida lightning storm focused us at its center. I focused my mind, my desires, my sexuality upon Johanna. Her body shimmering, her breathing no longer regular and steady, she walked to the bed that was separated from me by only the ottoman and another two feet of space. The storm, with buckets of rain, drowned her tapping on the hardwood floor.

Sitting on the bed, legs crossed in artistic display, she undid her bra and tossed it to the side. Smiling, with eyes never leaving mine, she massaged, explored, rubbed, and teased her breasts until the nipples were swollen, strained. She pinched and tugged with enough tension to streak desire between us. I knew that, from the wild look in her eyes, from the slightly bitten lips–hers and mine. No false displays for me. J captivated and aroused me with her sincerity of self-pleasuring.

I squirmed. I ached. I matched her ragged breathing with my own. I watched.

Rising from the edge of the bed, wedged between the bed, ottoman, and me, she was close enough to touch. Her perfume mingled with her desire, my desire, to form the smoke of a burning incense that swirled around us. Incense whose only purpose was to concentrate my gaze on the mandala of my Johanna. She towered above me in the heels, which she slowly slipped from her feet and placed by the bed. In one flowing motion, she undid the garter tabs, unfastened the belt, and held it securely in her hands as she sat upon the bed. Seductively, she concentrated on me as she tossed the belt aside, slipped the stocking from each leg and placed the nylons on the ottoman.

Slowly standing, and staring into my heart, she began to slide her thumbs along the waistband of her panties. At eye level, the black lace centered my attention to what was concealed. Her desire, her dampness had soaked the crotch. Bountiful pubic hair was outlined by her sweat and made a mosaic of texture clinging to the underside of the black silk. J's sensuality permeated the room. Spellbound, I didn't gaze at her eyes, but I knew they held the satisfaction of her display. She turned slightly, her cheek to my view and began a slow, tortuous descent of the silk (Had the Inquisition used this method, confessions would have been a piece of cake).

The panties edged downward. I edged to the front of my seat. Hands sweating, my fingers tensed. Sexual tension coursed through me, consumed me, set me afire. What beauty! Taut muscles outlined beneath smooth, smooth skin. The cheek of her ass quivered slightly as she tightened her pelvic muscles. Her crack was tantalizingly visible. The longer folds of her labia, moist and deepening red, peeked from below her crotch. She held from view her most exquisite mystery. When the panties found the floor, she stepped from them with pointed toes and tightening calves. Standing erect, she smoothed her hands from her waist down and around to her cheeks. I glanced up, then level. Her eyes closed in sensual concentration as she felt the fullness of her ass, hands slow and circling. I admired the rough red of her nails on that delicate kissable skin.

J turned to face me and sat on the bed with no inhibition, no timidity, only with the confidence of a beautiful woman in the most beautiful of situations. She lounged with left arm on the pillows, her left foot over the bedside almost touching the floor. The right foot, slender, delicate, dug into the sheet and bed to prop up her right leg. Widely exposed, she took no notice of me but studied and admired her entire body, her entire position. Her right hand traced a path from left shoulder to those luscious breasts. Seducing them with whispering fingertips, she again coaxed her nipples to hardness. The redness of her areola matched the polish of her nails–deep, dark, and invitingly sexual. Flashes of lightning silhouetted their texture and contrast to the smooth skin that kissed the outer edges of her nipples.

Down, down the fingers continued their route, across her abdomen, through the crease of her right leg and up, oh so slowly up, to the pinnacle of her knee. With fingers lingering on the kneecap, she looked at me, then back to their tactile journey. Down, oh so slowly down, she caressed toward her inner thigh. Fingertips became a rubbing palm across that sweet soft skin that can only be truly appreciated by the grazes of a lover's jaw.

As she eased her fingers across her mound of Venus, into the black, beckoning, wet hair, I became a fire that would only be extinguished by the dampness, the essence of Johanna. The storm crackled, poured, and jolted lightning sparks across the sky. J crackled with sexuality, poured visual delights from every pore, jolted my senses to the edge of endurance and sparked desire across my heart.

She closed her eyes in pleasure and swept practiced fingers among the folds of her labia. She caressed herself with instinctive moves and it gave up its secrets—warm, sweet juices that coated her fingers.

Deep inside she plunged her long, skilled fingers. How she maneuvered with such fingernails put me in awe. That suck-swish sound and the woman's tide she created was pure bliss. Again and again, slowly, with eons of patience, she pleasured herself, setting hips slightly in movement to help satisfy her needs. When she could take no more, when I could observe her loving no more, she slid those damp, perfumed fingers to her clitoris and rubbed, teased, and stroked her swelling, throbbing pearl to release. Only her low, primitive moans broke the stillness.

The storm front moved over. Gentle rain played upon the metal roof. The storm front she found in herself moved over her and me. Her gentle, satisfied gaze rested upon me. Mine reciprocated.

Laying her arm upon the propped knee, she casually beckoned me with a crooked, sexy forefinger that had just proved so capable. One of the fingers I wanted to lick. I knew my cue and hopped from the chair to take her in my arms. Her hand halted me.

"Your turn," she laughed with deadly seriousness.

"But I'm a dyke. I just wanted to watch you and get on to, well . . . *other* interests."

"Didn't you tell me in the car that you wanted to see all of me, no matter what?" She kept her pose on the bed.

"Well, yes," I had to agree.

"Well, so do I, Sweetheart. To see all of you is what I desire. All of your body, all of your heart, all of your mind–all of your true self."

I complied with that request of J's and many more she asked during the night. I learned some very astonishing things in the bed of that woman. Things that exploded my preconceived notions of butch/femme and lesbian sex.

She was a banshee of the tribade. She enjoyed using her tongue as much as I. She, like me, was a natural voyeur. She possessed a closet full of men's suits, another of dresses. She urged, coaxed, and demanded that I present my feminine and masculine sides in our lovemaking. There was no top vs. bottom, right vs. wrong, vanilla vs. S/M. There was only us–in all our sexual proclivities. That was enough to hold my heart and desires forever.

In the bed that was an island of our desires, she encircled me with arms and legs and had one last request before we drifted toward sleep. J wanted to know a secret–something none of my dyke friends knew.

Encircled in her warmth and security, I whispered it to her: "Embroidery. I've a passion for it."

"A wonderful revelation, Diane. Your true self," she whispered into my ear, then kissed me goodnight.

A few weeks later, at the Dairy Queen, sitting at a picnic table under moss-draped oaks, Johanna asked the fledgling dyke working there to snap our photo. The young woman was a natural (in more ways than one).

The picture captured our true selves, smiling at each other—me on the bench cradling her foot in my lap, stroking her tanned leg interrupted only by skimpy cutoffs; she sitting on the tabletop in her best pin-up girl pose. J said she'd keep the photo in her bedroom for my viewing pleasure.

Four months later we attended another cocktail party with John, family and associates. I mingled and observed. Johanna captivated and charmed. A new associate caught my attention from across the room. He moved over with a sway of style in his walk and masculine determination in his eyes. I admired his Italian suit. Definitely not purchased near here.

"You're Johanna's friend?" he queried, trying to become the center of my attention. "She's quite a wild pagan, isn't she?"

"No, quite an ordinary pagan but a very wild Hungarian gypsy," I replied, sipping my scotch and observing, beyond his shoulder, J with John across the room. She wore the black silk, different accessories, and her grandmother's silk shawl to ward off the slight chill of the evening.

He made small talk. "Do you have any hobbies, any nonprofessional interests?" Looking intense, he smiled seductively and arched an eyebrow.

"Oh, yes. I try to satisfy my visual addiction."

"Do you use brushes or pen and ink?" he asked seriously.

"Mostly my tongue, sometimes my hands, when the experience comes to a conclusion," I answered seriously,

sipping and continuing my admiration of J. He wasn't
John's most experienced associate. Tiring of me, he
sauntered on.

Our courtship twisted and turned with sexual
surprises and personal revelations into a relationship the
likes of which I never imagined possible. She stretched
my capabilities, my abilities to give love and receive it.
Johanna let me see the myriad of possibilities in the
sensuality that we are. She told me a million times in talks
from the trivial to the philosophical, "always be your
true self."

Years later, that were in essence too brief, on a
cold, low-hanging cloudy day, I stepped onto the porch
of Johanna's bungalow and rattled the key in the lock.
The day was barren and raw. My heart was barren and
raw. As I stepped into that house that mirrored my
sadness with its silence, a flood of tears ran down my
cheeks. They dropped with tiny taps of sound on the hardwood. Taps that echoed, I imagined, J's high heels and
the gaiety of her life in one focused, symbolic sound.

At the time I started my lonely, lonely walk through
the house, the storm front across the entire state witnessed
the circles of sorrow her death created.

In a large metropolitan city on the Gulf Coast, her
family sat in wake and beseeched with Catholic prayers
for her soul's salvation. Hearts devastated, lives put in
unthinkable chaos, they wept an ocean of tears that only
the Lady of Perpetual Sorrow might console.

In a mid-sized, geographically centered town,
John, family, and associates gathered at his house for their
good-byes. They stood on the veranda that J had loved,
where she danced so far into the nights, and drank a toast

to experiencing the beauty of her life. They sipped her favorite red wine and spoke of how each had loved her in a very different way.

In a small fishing village on the East Coast, my parents sat at a modest kitchen table and cried a river of tears. They offered Protestant prayers for my lover who had captured their hearts. Both considered Johanna my soulmate. They cried for me, the joy that I'd had and for what I may not have again. My Father's arm comforted my Mother's shoulder as she wiped her eyes with the hem of her cobbler's apron.

I couldn't join any circle. Mine was a suffering encompassing one.

Determined to complete my task, I gathered my books and clothes and loaded them into the car. Taking one last walk through the house, I complied with J's Mother's request to take whatever I desired. Our joint possessions of the house held no interest for me.

Entering the bedroom, I sensed her. I gazed at the bed and expected her to seduce me toward it with a sexy smile and provocative pose. I gathered a few material things–our picture at the Dairy Queen; her grandmother's shawl; from the jewelry box, her sorority ring and diamond I'd given her; and from the dresser, the beautiful filigreed barrette that she'd unclasp to allow that sexy, unbound hair to bring excitement to my heart.

Locking the door, I placed the key in her next-door neighbor's keeping for her Mother. I took one last look–to lock all her memories in my heart for a lifetime.

I slipped a tape into the player. "Anticipation" began, but I felt no joy in my favorite song. I anticipated nothing. Tears falling in time to the rhythm, I headed for the river.

Five years later, in another part of the state, at a cocktail party for the academically inclined, I surveyed the room. Pleasant chit-chat surrounded me. No one caught my eye. Someone brushed my shoulder.

"Excuse me, but isn't that a 19th century shawl from Eastern Europe? The fringed knotwork is exquisite."

That was quite a come-on line but precisely correct. "Why, yes. How did you know? No one knows *that*." I spoke while turning my gaze to discover a woman in a crisp, smartly tailored linen suit.

"Textiles. I've a passion for textiles."

"Anything else you might have a passion for?" I inquired as I gently, but seductively, rubbed her sleeve to admire the material and to signal my emotion.

"Automobiles."

The image of her splayed on a mechanic's creeper in far less than a linen suit was delightful.

Perhaps ten years my senior, the handsome stranger stirred a tinge of fateful compatibility in my heart.

"And yourself . . . your interests?"

"Many and varied, but I always try to be my true self."

She slowly admired me up and down, with appreciation. "Then our possibilities are endless. Perhaps you'd care for dinner in a slightly, shall we say, more romantic environment. Somewhere truly befitting that beautiful dress, stylish heels, and priceless shawl."

As she spoke she reached to lightly touch and feel the texture of my filigreed barrette. She had a dyke heart and appreciated the visual.

I accepted.

Chapter Seven

My Kindred Sister

I left my house today on a very short walk. My cousin, Abigail, lives about eight houses down the road from me. She'd asked my help at a party she was giving at her home. We're both of such a somewhat, shall I say, independent nature that we seldom ask for help. I jumped at the opportunity to be of assistance and gladly began my journey toward her house. It was a beautiful Florida winter day; the kind folks in the North dream about during the fifth heavy snow of the year. It began as such a common event. It ended with some astounding revelations into my life–things I had never quite put in the perspective they deserved.

Abigail and I are a generation apart. We both grew up and now live in the same tiny fishing village that our relatives settled about seventy years ago. It's a tiny spot (if you can find it at all on the map), but it's an area of Northeast Florida on the St. Johns River that is so beautiful I hate to leave it to go to town. I call it paradise (though growth is happening and changing it into an integral part of the county), a place that holds my roots, my history, my extended relatives and cousins in assorted degrees of nearness. A place that I traveled from, feeling that the "big outside" must be better. A place that pulled me back, because I am truly only myself where my heart is peaceful. For me, that's the River.

Of all the brothers, sisters, aunts, uncles, and cousins in my realm of relativity, I feel the closest affinity with Abigail. I never put people in descriptive boxes or label them. It's not my nature. I will tell you that I consider her a Sister of the Inclination. She and I have an eye for the same type of relationships, for the preferred company of women, and we both possess a rather stubborn, independent, but reserved, temperament that often lesbian feminists are noted for. In my case, it's a true reading of myself. For Abigail and me, generally speaking, I'll chalk up the stubborn, extremely reserved portion of our similarities to our inherited O'Reilly temperament. The highest compliment I can tell you about my cousin, how we mirror and touch each other's true essences, is that I consider her to be my kindred sister.

Stepping out into my driveway toward her home, I thought about my earliest memories of Abigail. I was five. My Mother, her aunt, went with Abigail's parents to Tallahassee for her graduation from Florida State University. Believe me, times and social assumptions were very different in the early '50s. It was a *big* deal, by our small village standards. My Mother talked of nothing else for weeks before and nothing of more importance in the years that followed. I learned from her that the phrase "Abigail's graduation" meant a way out of the ordinary, a way out of having only the option of early marriage, and a way to "use your potential" (I was nine before I really got that word's significant meaning, but my Mother spoke it almost with such reverence, I knew at five and six it was a phrase to be remembered).

Through my elementary school years, I got so caught up in the wonderful universe and endless possibilities that education and access to libraries opened to me, that Abigail physically slipped from my existence. Mentally, she was always as close as the dreams that are so abundant in our youth. I'd sit on our porch swing and read. As my Mother sat in her favorite chair, crocheting her most exquisite works of art, she'd glance over once in a while and remind me, "Just like your cousin Abigail. Such a student; such a reader. You're going to do great things, Di." My Mother said it with such assurance that, as a shy, often reclusive, very eccentric little kid living in a world where families struggled from paycheck to paycheck, I confidently believed her.

When I was 12, Abigail jolted into the reality of my intense (and emerging lesbian-leaning) observations of the world. Her Father's accidental drowning in the River recalled her and her husband, Franklin, from Formosa. I'd already begun my obsession with really studying, noting the subtle actions and personalities of the people around me. It just made me quieter and more shy. I have to be silent to do the observing. Some people don't.

She struck me with her independence, straightforwardness, and her take-charge abilities, but I felt that she was also a double-edged sword. There was something reserved, something not put before everyone, that was so much like me. I wanted to shout about it. I did not. Social norms–and the ability to walk their tightropes of compliance–are learned very early in the South. One can bear a lot here, except true social disgrace. I kept quiet but watched and admired this woman who touched my heart with an unspoken, subtly perceived glint of mirrored recognition.

As I began my walk in earnest, turning north from my driveway, I suddenly recalled a moment when I was seventeen years old. Prophetic moments are often so casual, so fleeting, we lose them in the business of our lives. This moment is sharp and clear. It cuts to the core of my true self with its revelation. I think about it often, when I study the journey of my life.

In this mind flash, I am in the kitchen with my Mother, standing at our sink and observing the view of the River through the kitchen windows in front of me. I'm not supposed to be observing but peeling potatoes. My Mother is stirring a pot on the stove and waiting for the spuds.

We'd talked about little stuff, things that occurred at school, how she did the wash that day, how my Aunt Eileen was feeling better after her cold. My Mother suddenly starts talking about Abigail and her friend, Dorothy. Just chit-chat about a get-together (planned for the house I'm now walking toward). I suddenly have a lot of unspoken feelings that find their escape through tears that fall into the bowl in the sink with the potato peelings.

I want you to know my Mother loved me, but she never quite knew what to do with me. This was certainly one of those moments.

"Di," she observed, turning from the cooking pot with the wooden spoon still in her hand, "you can worry about something forever. It won't change the way you are. You're going to graduate and soon be on your way to college. Your Dad and I are so proud. You're going to make something of yourself." She paused and stared me down with her Irish blue eyes that burned holes into my soul when she set her mind to it. "You're going to be just like Abigail."

I was electrified by my Mother's observation. She and I both knew that her reference was to much, much more than the academic inclination she usually meant. This time, she described the inclination of my heart. She got the verb tense wrong; "going to be" should have been "you are" period. My Mother wasn't aware (I hoped) about the gaiety of life I'd discovered and found I had a natural passion for. I was, as they say now, "outed" by my Mother's words.

I knew with certainty she wouldn't want to know the details. All I could say in response was, "You're absolutely right."

My path was struck. My karmic destiny, with all the wonderful women it would contain, was set before me. For the love, the wonderment, the exquisiteness of life my path has given me, I often say blessings for my Mother's words–and for Abigail.

Glancing to my left, through the yards of houses that have been built in our small village during my lifetime, I gaze at the beauty of the River that always captivates me, always fills me with such serenity and inspiration. Regardless if it is storm-tossed or crystal glass,

I never drink in its strength, its life-force, enough. A breeze, slightly crisp, without the humidity of summer, catches my cheek. No cars pass on the road, and my steps could be taken with my eyes closed.

It's so true, Abigail and I have a lot in common. To say I admire her would be a true statement, but it would not reach the finer, more detailed point of how she has touched my life. She has been a thread, a constant, a mentor in many ways, but always, much more deeply, she has held my eye of observation, respect, and love, because she is my kindred sister.

Our academic pursuits, though in different areas and situations, are probably the striking similarities that most of our families see. Now retired, she has worked as both teacher and principal. That takes discipline, organization, determination, and perseverance. Those are traits I admire in her, as well as in myself. Where Abigail balanced an academic professional career and personal life with such expenditure of emotional energy, I would not choose to do so. Circumstance and situation would turn me away from the academic life of postgraduate publishing and scholastic research. In a way, as I look at it now, it was a blessing. I do not possess her grit and guts to balance both–the private with the public, the beyond the ordinary with the mundane. She has that confidence. I admire her for that . . . but I fear she has paid too high a price in emotional peace of mind during those years and times when the societal norm was maintained regardless of the private torment. I could not do it. She is a strong-willed, gutsy woman.

During that time, when social pressures were much more demanding, much more the law of the everyday,

Abigail married. I believe she and Franklin, without the marriage, would have been the best of friends. With the marriage, Abigail's persuasion to the inclination, and other circumstances, there was divorce. I watched this, growing up. When those around me often saw it as such a sad situation, I noticed more. I saw an independent woman who could take care of herself and her child. I saw a woman who did not abide by general rules or bend to commented urgings. I also saw a situation that I did not want for myself. Abigail's divorce, regardless of the private motive, was a public declaration for me that solidified my natural inclinations against contrasting, though slightly changing, public attitudes. I would not follow the matrimonial path, though the offer would be proposed. She gave me the strength of exampled independence. For that, I bless her.

We both have children, though in slightly different ways. I watched Abigail raise her child after her divorce and was struck by some things–things I've never truly spoken to her about. Things that I believed whisper so close to her, and to my true self, that forming an observation on them has remained solely mine, without comment from anyone.

I believe that Abigail holds a great deal of personal conflict because she has a child and is of the persuasion. I believe she feels you can't have both. That's my observation. In this area, we are very different, probably due to the cultural times that have shaped our individual personal philosophies and us. I want to talk about that with her someday–to let her know that I truly do believe you can have the best of all possible worlds. You can experience the nurturing, the raising, the enfolding of the mystery of a child growing into adulthood. You can also be blessed with the mystery of most exquisite proportions–that defies our small words and imposed cultural norms–the wonderment, the sacredness, of women who love women.

Though I think that this area of my cousin's life has brought her much conflict at times, it has also given me much courage–courage to undertake the raising of my daughter becoming her legal mother through single-parent adoption. It was a long, torturous journey to that legal recognition. It has been a journey well worth the sacrifice. I don't think those who associate with us would put either of us at the top of the Mother category. I don't believe people perceive us that way. That we raised daughters, that we both did it with our own values, style, and grace–regardless of what the norm might be–for that I think we are to be proud. Both children grew with love and independence, blessings bestowed on them by virtue of our very extraordinary lives.

A single car passes and I wave. It's a neighbor down the road. This is a very small place. Everyone knows everyone and everything.

While Abigail and I have both held in our lives relationships with women, we have dealt with them in somewhat different ways. During the years that I finished junior and senior high school and moved on to college, Abigail had a very close friend, Dorothy. I saw a lot in that situation. A few years later, I would see a lot of that situation in me. Oh, people talk, people assume, and people can gossip, but I've always been of the opinion that all of that is the outside. What is truly the inside is what touches your heart. That's how I feel to this day about Abigail and Dorothy. I sensed that whatever else the situation held for them, it held a great deal of control and negative bonding for Abigail. That's my observation. I'm sure she might give you an entirely different perspective. Please remember that her heart was on the inside. Please remember, also, that I hold such a protective concern for her that it may have clouded my perceptions.

Their relationship and my study of it touched my life during those years in two very significant ways. First, it persuaded me that I would divide (or strongly attempt to do so) my life into two separate spheres—one that was the outside, my work, my school, my family, my straight friends, and one that was my inside, the one that touched my heart, my relationship with Johanna. I was consumed by love for that beautiful woman, but I was also consumed by the pain, the denial, the struggle to hide the obvious in the daily straightness of life that I had seen Abigail endure.

I wanted the best of both worlds but didn't know how to attain it to a theoretical, satisfactory conclusion in the merging of my existences. I know everyone lives a distinct life, but I learned from Abigail, or so I thought at the time, that the small, small place that contained our lives held no room for successfully combining both situations, without torturous endeavors of mind and heart.

Second, as I struggled to keep my situations clean and distinct, I struggled with college and required grades. I struggled to keep Johanna from totally consuming my waking hours as she consumed my nights. I struggled with the passion of our togetherness that made me soar beyond the small village by the River. I struggled with the inability to bring who I loved to the place I loved. I struggled with my inability to control or resolve my struggles. When I lacked the strength to struggle more, but still everything remained the same and tortured my soul, I drank.

That which I saw in Abigail's relationship and dreaded for its destructive force, I now mirrored in my own. The reasons for it may have been very different but the alcohol had the same effect upon our lives. It drew out the worst of the demons that we possessed in our O'Reilly temperament and magnified them until we were chained to a habit that only the superhuman are able to overcome. That we have both subdued it, I consider a miracle of sorts. The law of averages should destine one of us to fail. Abigail's consumption was a tad more open than mine, but I believe mine was the most truly destructive. It was done in private, mostly in the dark of night, when Johanna would not come to me (Poetically, it was my dark side in the dark of night that produced only a gulf of darkness between my lover and me). I unleashed the most wicked, unresolved terrors of my heart with the scotch I would consume, but I had another terrible secret, which drove me to more . . . more scotch, more heartache, more of an inability to draw close to the love of my life. I enjoyed the act of drinking. I think it's easier to subdue if you truly don't love it.

My cousin and I struggled. To me, there was a drawing-together of our wills by the subduing of the alcohol that consumed us. It's another kindred secret I've never shared with her.

I'm almost within sight of her house. No traffic. A beautiful day. I glance again at the River.

There's a phrase in German that I truly love–von Anderen Uffer, "from the other side of the water, of the river, of the shore." It's a term that describes someone who doesn't belong. It's more. It's a straight term that describes someone who is gay or lesbian. I like it because it combines two proclivities that are so much an integral, basic part of me–my life that is not quite the ordinary, with the element of water, the River. I think it mirrors a lot of me–my uniqueness, my not denying that I'm a tad socially, psychologically, politically, maybe even genetically, different with my love, my pull toward this River that I live by. This water influences a lot of my writing– especially my poetry. Maybe it's because I'm fated, as a Pisces, that I so love it.

Sometimes, I think it is that, but also something more; something that is genetically linked through primitive time and memories to a sense of longing for, a sense of having, a sense of centeredness, that manifests itself in the grounding and love of place–the River. To describe it in Abigail is for you to see it also in me.

Abigail is a lover of place, of home, of situations that are steady and unchanging. She is also a lover of the River. A lot of people live by it, but few truly notice it, see it for the ever-changing beauties that are caught in the constant, the certainty, the sureness of its flow. She is a much more accomplished fisherwoman than I, but her love of place is much deeper than that. She never fails to admire, to cherish every sunset that passes, every bank of storm clouds that pull from the southwest and bring thunderstorms in the summer, and every change of tide or current that marks the rhythm of a fisherman's day.

It is not just the River that catches her talented eye. She loves critters, large and small and has a knowledge of birds that I will never acquire in two lifetimes. Her yard, with its ancient live oak trees, is adorned with birdhouses and feeding stations. There's a feeder right outside her kitchen window that combines her admiration and interest in birds with the most exquisite view of the River. It's the best of all worlds. It's her true self.

Her house is as unique and interesting as she is (a story in itself). It's a true living museum that surrounds her with bits of the past and blends with her and her partner's interests to create a kaleidoscope of situations frozen in time. It's in her house that I first tasted what became my lasting love of the Oriental. It's in her house that I can admire handmade cast nets, works of true art that are both beautiful and functional. It's in her house that I hold my link to our shared past. She tells me of incidents, of family members, happenings from long before my birth.

I'm approaching the yellow, two-story house next to hers. The yard is stunning. Hibiscus is still in bloom. This is the house where Abigail grew up. Her sister lives there now. Across the street, her niece has built a new home. It's a small place. All our lives and relationships are in some way intertwined. We're all drawn here by our love of place and links to the past that give us strength.

When I was thirty-six, I decided to leave this small place for the "big outside." You know that saying about the grass being greener. Well, for me, leaving did destine me to find my partner, but it also destined me to know such a sadness I thought I would be unable to endure. It was the first time in my life that I lost my true sense of place, of feeling in the right situation. Time passed before we moved back. I think my partner did it because she holds such a love for me that she could no longer take the darkness that daily grew thicker in my soul, my actions, my desires, and in my melancholy, poet-steeped temperament. She calls that aspect of me–my moody, Irish, brooding, self–my O'Reilly side. She's right.

I think Abigail holds a lot of that O'Reilly side–that which can conjure up emotional demons and bouts of distancing in our souls to such a degree that we are hard to touch or to console. I hope when she returned home, as I did, that she vowed never to take our love of place, our love of the River, for granted. It's a vow I sincerely made and keep every day, to the best of my ability.

When I began my journey to the "big outside," Abigail was one of the last people I spoke to in Florida. She was the only one who wished me well on my "wonderful adventure."

My partner and I returned to Florida four years later. We did not settle initially by the River but thirty miles north in a large city. I was changed in many, many ways. Circumstance and my partner's nervous breakdown had brought avenues so unexpected.

When I saw Abigail again, she was changed in many ways. Dorothy had passed away, Abigail had retired, alcohol no longer consumed her, and there was something else, something more I could not quite put my finger on. It was something that gave her a more comfortable presence–a smoothing, oh, so subtly, of our O'Reilly side. I knew immediately what the something was when she and her sister sat at our dining room table munching on fried chicken one night at supper. It only took two words, dropped matter-of-factly, casually, in the conversation–Miss Eleese. None of us missed a beat in the rhythm of dining, but I decided right then and there that a woman who could inspire such a change in my kindred sister had my immediate, unseen approval. Instantly, she became my cousin-in-law. My partner had Abigail's assurance, before she left, that we'd soon get together with Miss Eleese.

Theirs is a truly destined relationship. I hope, someday, they'll give me their story in all its details. I want to write the words of their togetherness.

I step from the road upon the winding gravel path that leads to Abigail's house. Growing up in this yard and house, feeling the familiarity that slowly enfolds me as I make my way toward her, I truly feel at home, at peace . . . comfortable and welcome. Sometimes that's a feeling hard for me to attain. The insecurities of the haunting sadness of my Irish self often get in the way.

As I reach for the back door handle, I reach some conclusions–conclusions that maybe the perspective of age has finally allowed me to organize and coalesce.

I admire my cousin Abigail for so much. Much more than she'll ever know, but what I feel for her is deeper, stronger. I respect her, what she has done with her life and in her life. She has given me courage, example, and inspiration. I'm such an independent person; few do I allow to be true mentors to me. She is the only one I've allowed to be everything to me–someone I've admired and learned from professionally and on a personal level.

As she comes to the door and is happy to see me–to see me as my true self–I decide it's time. It's time to reveal a part of my, oh, so reserved heart. It's time she should know, through the flow of my words, that she is my kindred sister.

Chapter Eight

Christmas Déjà Vu

As the lights dim, the tiny church in the village where I live is filled with darkness that can't hide the increasing expectation of parents and grandparents or the focusing of many in the congregation on a ritual that is comfortable and sure, but always new, and hidden with surprises. I sit beside my cousin, Abigail, and am torn between two possibilities.

Do I stay in the moment and discover the simplicity that bursts with meaning or do I wander mentally to the time I saw a miracle–the time I saw Jesus get a kiss?

I decide, as the antique and just slightly (though not to annoyance) out-of-tune piano sounds the final eight bars of a holiday Protestant hymn, that I can do both. Be in the here and now *and* on a Christmas Eve I won't ever forget–1975. There's a lot of tradition, relationships, and meaning gathering in the tiny thirty by forty-five foot room that is this block church, unadorned and very utilitarian (Martin Luther and John Wesley would both be pleased with the unpretentious style of the building that holds those tonight who are unpretentious and straightforward in their beliefs).

There's a lot of broken and expanded tradition in me–a lot of newfound relationships and not quite so conventional disciplines of thought and action. In me, there're a lot of new ways to realize a different meaning. As we rise for the minister's invocation, I stand close to my cousin but feel distanced from the relatives around me. I will not remain hidden in this circle of congregates, and I'm a little on edge at breaking all the Protestant rules in such a, shall we say, extreme religious setting. I'm ill-at-ease, not for myself, but for those around me. It's not often these folks are beset by such a blatant Sister of the Inclination, in the fifth pew, right-hand side of the church, at the Christmas Pageant service, four days before Christmas.

It's not often that I become such a symbol of their wayward sinner in the worst degree. Believe me, a division of the wheat and the chaff is alive and well in Riverdale, Florida. My Sisters of the Tribe who read this: I am not the prodigal's daughter being welcomed home with open arms. I think that sums up the mood of the folks around me and myself, as the minister reaches the "Amen" part.

To understand the angst that stirs a tad in me, you must know that the seat I occupy when we sit after the "Amen" is the seat I grew up in. The seat occupied by my family, long passed over. The seat I occupied and formed my different view of existence as ministers came and went, and as bylaws and official views of the church became more specific, less liberal, less encompassing of that which is different–less like me. The seat I finally gave up when I could no longer deny my true self.

My cousin, who is also of the Persuasion, retaliates from the norm in a different way. She occupies this pew, with her partner, every Sunday and shows that we are everywhere. She shows that we are steadfast and caring members of our churches and communities, that we will not be denied. We come from slightly opposite ends of the spectrum of Sisterhood. She blends, I'm more blatant. She perseveres, I protest. She is the thread of conventionality, I'm the scissors that try to keep that thread very short.

As we sit and the Sunday school director welcomes one and all to the Christmas program, my cousin squeezes my hand and whispers, "It's so good to have you here. It's been too long, Diane."

I nod in agreement. Tears slip down my cheek. "Thanks," I reply. She's right. It's good to be here. Good not to let a part of me slip away, because I've moved beyond these ritualized and rule-filled beliefs. Good to remember and refresh the roots that are my family and faith.

I settle and remind myself that all things are part of the whole. All differences become similar in the circle that turns us. Here is my home. Here's where I truly saw an auspicious sign.

Always the church's Christmas Story is directed and prepared by the Sunday school classes. When I was a child, my Mother was in charge of costuming the productions. Between Thanksgiving and the night of the pageant, our front and dining rooms took on the feel of a theater backstage. When I was small, I'd watch my Mother turn bits of bent coat hangers, elastic, semi-stiff white, small-weave netting, glue and glitter, into the most beautiful angel wings imaginable. Bits of saved trim, remnants of sewing, odd buttons and discarded stickpins blended with strips of muslin to become regal headdresses for wise men.

When I grew older, I sat on a living room footstool, held *Children's Stories of Jesus* on my lap, and discussed with my Mother just why people in the Holy Land never seemed to have need of hip-waders or work gloves. I also pondered that their fishing techniques were very primitive, compared to my Dad's skiff and nets. As my Mother matched flannel bathrobes and rope waist ties with children of assorted sizes, she said it was the "spirit of the times" that made the Hold Land of the book so different from us.

While still very young I learned to appreciate cultural differences. My Mother always told me to note the wrapping of shawls and turbans, to study how sandals in the pictures were so simple, but functional, for the deserts, which inspired the Hebrew prophets to religious awakenings. Nothing of artistic beauty or detail in the pictures escaped my Mother's discerning eye. I bless her for giving me this gift. Appreciation of detail is a trait of mine that I try to enhance daily.

My Dad was also drawn into these community productions. Usually, other fathers in the community made primitive palm-frond-draped backdrops and mangers that yearly changed in size and form, as production needs demanded. Dad, not having a true talent for carpentry, always made the staffs for the shepherds and Joseph. When I was young, they were usually odd broomsticks, scraped of paint, and given thin strokes with his pocket-knife to simulate wear and tear. He and I discussed one year, as we sat on the dock, and he cut thin shavings off the broom handles, that neither he nor I had ever seen a staff for sheep. He told me that was what "watching their flocks by night" meant. As a boy in Illinois, he recalled the next farm over had sheep; but nobody, as he could recollect, ever used a staff. The year I was ten, my Dad (at my Mother's insistence that we never had true staffs that looked like the ones with crooked ends in the picture book with well-worn pages) took his task to heart. He began, nightly, to put on his reading glasses and study the book for a few minutes after supper. At the end of the week, he gave me a goodnight hug and kiss when I was ready to head to bed.

He said, "We're having real shepherds' crooks in the Christmas play this year, my snookiwacky." My Dad always called me snookiwacky when he kissed me goodnight.

That was the week after Thanksgiving. My Dad scoured the woods around our house for the perfect oak branches. When he finished at work, and before supper, he would sit on the dock and work on the crooks. The early sunsets made his work time short, and he worked every evening until Mom would have me run and fetch him. The week of the big pageant, my Dad walked from the dock, when I got him for supper, holding my hand and letting me use one of the four staffs he'd made. He carried the other three, balanced on his shoulder with his free hand.

I bounded to the back porch and my Dad stood by the porch steps, waiting for my Mother. Leaning my staff by the back door, I dashed through the door to get her from the kitchen. She slowly pushed the back screen open and wiped her hands on her apron. The scene I caught at that moment was one that reminded me of stories about their courting that they would relate to me growing up. Just as my very seemingly unromantic Dad had presented flowers to Miss Gladys on the front porch steps, this evening, as she stepped, work-tired, from the kitchen, he presented her with one of the staffs. All she said, as she had the years before, was "Well, I'll be, Dudley! How beautiful!"

My Dad beamed as she ran her beautiful hands over the whittled and trimmed branches that were graced with curves that made true crooks on the staffs. He had oiled the wood, and they looked like staffs, well worn and passed from generation to generation of families from the picture book who watched those flocks.

She leaned over the edge of the porch and gave him a kiss. Not a peck on the cheek but a real movie-type kiss that they held for a long, long moment. Their demonstrations of affection were not extremely blatant, but when I witnessed them I knew they were true and sincere. It's a moment frozen in time I'll never forget. A moment, whose love and intimacy I wish I could find, just as true and sincere, in my own life.

I'm pulled back to the moment, as garbed shepherds make their way down the center aisle of the tiny church, toward Mary and Joseph sitting on the minister's platform. Smiling, I remember how my grade-school cousins would vie for the role of shepherd. Wise men were just so-so, as I grew up. Shepherds were the roles to get, because you got to go barefoot. Everyone went barefoot in summertime, but our Moms were strict about shoes in winter. Being a shepherd meant you could show your toughness.

The last shepherd, also the oldest, carried one of my Dad's staffs. It was a comforting sight to see. Eight shepherds–eight boys, six to eleven. The church was growing.

Angels in more assorted sizes and ages than the shepherds made their entrance. The littlest held her sister's hand. They were stunning and sparkly in white gowns with splendid wings and haloes of tinsel that gleamed in the candlelight. The tinsel was formed into circular crowns that were placed on their combed, shiny hair, instead of held above them like Renaissance paintings. Slow and serious, they made their way down the aisle. Were the older ones thinking of storybook weddings that would trace tonight, with slow and serious steps and gowns of white, down this same aisle in perhaps eight to ten years?

There was a new twist in the angelic host. The Mom of three small cherubs with wings brought up the flock of winged spirits. She played the archangel and also served as spiritual guide and overseer of behavior when they took their seated positions on benches behind Mary, Joseph, and Baby Jesus. They smiled and giggled just a little and waved to their families in the audience. They were happy angels. All must be right in heaven.

The congregation sang "We Three Kings," as three grown men with natural beards walked the center aisle and laid gifts before the manger. Tall, elegant, and solemn, their costuming was beautiful. Silk scarves twisted into turbans. Robes were fashioned with flowing sleeves from several types of metallic-patterned material. Sashes were abstract and eye-catching. They wore wrapped leggings of orange, yellow and white. Shoes were black house slippers, with splashes of colored sequins. Someone in the congregation carried on the art of theatrical design. No detail had been overlooked. Gold necklaces and silver medallions adorned them. Fingers were gypsied with many bright-stoned rings and all wore a single dangling earring. They looked mysterious, luxuriant, and rich. Perfect wise men bearing gifts. Strings of electric twinkling lights blinked behind the Nativity scene.

Abigail leaned to me and whispered, "Not enough older boys to play the parts, but they look good, don't they?"

"Sure do," I whispered back.

I knew the ritual and the program. After the wise men entered, we would sing one more song, "Joy to the World," and the minister would give us benediction, before all retired to the fellowship/Sunday school room for refreshments.

We rose to sing, as the piano player presented the first few introductory bars. My cousin held the songbook and began to sing. I surveyed the peaceful holiday scene. Candlelight gleamed from the six stained glass sanctuary windowsills and sent kaleidoscopes of warm rainbow shadows through the room. Pine sprays cradling each candle sent aromatic streams of natural rustic beauty through the church. It smelled and felt like Christmas in this place. It felt like a holiday season to be celebrated with family and friends. I knew the home-baked cookies and pies waiting in the fellowship hall would be just as aromatic and holiday evoking as the natural, fresh-cut pine.

Closing my eyes, I took in all that swirled around me. How the smells, the sounds, the ambiance of the situation paralleled the solstice celebration I had attended the second week of December. Symbols were different, but they both had a similar, almost archetypical feel. Universal truth mirrored in the myriad facets of prismatic symbols.

As we sang the second verse, I went back in time— back to 1975. It was the year I broke from this church, because of my lesbianism and my growing Wiccan beliefs. That was the holiday season that marked the great turning changes in my life. I began the process of deep, deep change in my heart and the steps toward my true self and my true philosophies.

I prayed to the Goddess, as I dressed my god-child as a cherub with beautiful coat hanger wings my Mother had made. She was three, bright, very articulate (as she still is) and looking forward to her part in the play more than Santa Claus. Gudrun insisted that every fold, every flow of her designed-to-fit pillowcase gown, with flowing sleeves (the remaining portion of the pair) and V-neckline trimmed in gold bias tape fit perfectly. The gold bracelet that she always wore was adjusted properly on her wrist, and her white Mary Janes were buckled just so, and her gold socks had precisely folded cuffs (She was definitely picking up my Mother's eyes of style and sartorial detail).

As my Dad helped her into her wings, sprinkled with glittering angel dust, she beamed with a beauty and a smile I will never forget. Sitting on my Dad's knee, she struck her best angelic pose, and I crouched behind them and put my arms around both pairs of shoulders. My Mother snapped the Kodak moment as she said how lovely we all looked. My Dad and I knew the "lovely" was meant for Gudrun-the angel of all our hearts, even without the wings.

She hugged and kissed my Mother and me good-bye, before she walked the short distance to the church with my Dad. We figured the short walk would expend some excessive three-year-old energy and give my Dad an errand he loved–taking Gudrun anywhere. She had become the second generation Snookiwacky–the second generation to hold his strong, callused hand and feel safe and loved.

Loading the last minute nativity props into the trunk, I waited to drive my Mother down the road. She locked our front door with one hand, held Gudrun's Baby Alive under the other arm and held her purse in that hand. The doll was missing her usual pink dress, socks, and Mary Janes. She was dressed like the cherub Gudrun, minus wings and footwear.

At the church, as children grouped in the fellow-ship hall for last words of instruction, my Dad and a few other men arranged final details on the manger and Nativity backdrop and placed fresh straw on the minister's platform for effect. Church friends, relatives, grandparents and parents of pageant participants combined with the usual congregation to fill the pews to overflowing. My Mother patted down the straw in the manger, placed the doll with angelic face inside and hurried to the fellowship hall for a final costume check. I found my godparents and my Mother Holtsinger and hugged and kissed them all.

Whispering that I'd sit with them later in the fellowship hall, I hurried to the back of the church to find a place to stand. As the lights dimmed and the minister called us all to prayer, I squeezed between two second cousins, behind the last pew on the right-hand side.

The minister prayed. I prayed also for a sign that pulling from my religious roots and toward my Wiccan proclivities was the right path. If unobtrusive, my lesbianism was tolerated in this small place. To show what I really was—a lesbian who would no longer blend, and a Wiccan—would shatter my world, my family. I was determined, this solstice season, that I would bring it all out in the open—to live every day, every situation, every moment as my true self. It was a big step, with irreparable consequences. I prayed for a sign that it was the right one.

The pageant went off with perfect precision—if such can really be said of twenty kids between three and thirteen years of age. With no major part, Gudrun still stole all our hearts with her presence, her captivating charm. At the end of the program, after the lights brightened, the minister invited all to fellowship in the annex.

Remaining silent, the audience waited patiently for the actors to leave the stage, exiting the church's rear side door into the Sunday school area. In the rules of childhood, they naturally left in single file and in pecking order—older and larger first. Gudrun was standing by my third cousin, Leslie, who was also an angel, but about ten years old. Gudrun waved to my Mom and Dad, then to my godparents and blew a kiss to Mother Holtsinger, as she waited to get in the departing line of Mary, Joseph, wise men, shepherds and angels. During the program, she wasn't near the manger. A kneeling shepherd blocked her view. She'd been content to hold Leslie's hand and pat one of my nephews (also a shepherd) on the back and hug his neck during bored moments of hymn singing. He loved it, as he considered himself, at nine and a half, her self-appointed, chivalrous protector. She was content and happy in this make-believe world of special dress-up. Friends and playmates surrounded her.

As the line moved out the door, Leslie took her place and Gudrun, the last of this wonderful biblical procession, followed almost on cue. Crossing behind the manger, she glanced toward it, then stopped and placed both her hands on the wooden crib rail. She stared at the baby, as the actors, concerned with refreshments and praise, left the room. The audience remained silent and seated as the amazing scene unfolded. Gudrun, oblivious to us all, studied the Baby Jesus, then reached down and felt the doll's cheek and ran her small plump hand over the white pillowcase remnant robe that was accented with gold bias tape at neck and sleeves, playing through the straw with her fingers. Her eyes never left the doll's face. She smiled and stood on tiptoe, with the fingers of both hands tightly curled on the edge of the crib for balance, and gave the Baby Jesus a tender kiss on the cheek. The sound of it was angel soft.

The audience let out a collective sigh of emotion and no one moved. Tears filled my eyes and those of many others. My Mother Holtsinger wiped her cheek with a fresh hanky. The room was silent with anticipation.

Gudrun scooped up the baby and searched the audience for something. Electricity filled the room. The spirituality that was evoked was greater than that of any sermon I'd ever heard, and it swirled around us all.

Smiling, with the baby in her arms—a cherub matching a cherub—she bounded from the platform, searched the smiling faces again, and walked happily down the red indoor/outdoor-carpeted center aisle toward the back of the room. All heads turned to follow her progress and unknown route.

Halfway down the carpet, she giggled, clutched the Baby Jesus tighter in preparation for really running, and took off with a giggle for every pounce of her Mary Janes on the carpet. I instinctively bent to my knees and held out my arms when I realized I was the end of the journey.

She yelled, as she found my waiting embrace, "Di, Di, she's the Baby Jesus!" As I picked her up, she gave the baby a kiss, then smacked me with a similar wet smooch.

I smooched her back and felt my sign had been given. I snuggled her close and gave a similar smooch to Baby Jesus, caught protectively between us.

Again, the minister said a few words about the wonderful program and ended with a loud "Amen."

I knew, at that moment, I'd witnessed a miracle. The Goddess had set my path when the girl of my heart brought the Jesus that was a *she* to me. All things are part of the whole. All differences become similar in the circle that turns us.

We end the closing hymn and the minister dismisses us with an "Amen" returned by the congregation. As we start to file out the church's main double door and head toward the fellowship hall and refreshments, my cousin Abigail embraces my shoulder and asks, "Bring back memories, Diane? We've seen a lot of these programs together."

"Sure does, and we sure have," I reply.

"Not as spectacular as the night Jesus got a kiss, eh?"

I was startled–believing the act had had impact only on me. Tears filled my eyes and I wiped them with a fresh hanky, as we stepped into the crisp winter night that held a thousand star lights like those that had just twinkled behind Mary and Joseph.

"It's a night that changed my life, Abigail, only for the best."

"I know," she said, as she walked with me toward the fellowship hall. "She certainly has been an inspiration for you."

I glanced at her in the light of the hall porch as she winked and grinned, "The Baby Jesus, I mean, of course."

"Of course," I, knowing better, agreed as I held the door for her.

Chapter Nine

The Fish Woman

I've always loved the water–especially the ocean. Maybe it's because my Dad was a fisherman. Maybe it's because I'm a Pisces. Whatever the reason, the ocean captivates me. It lures me with sensuality and mystery. That's the reason I try to be near it, or in it, whenever I can. That's the reason I'm sitting at the Pagoda pool on an early spring day–a day so beautiful even the sky is envious of the blue of the ocean which holds my gaze.

For some reason, as I rest in the poolside lounger, I start to think about my Dad. Something he first said as I helped him pull in nets when I was a child, haunts my thoughts, "Always use good bait and pull the fish gently. That way the fish will catch you."

As a child, I'd overlooked the phrasing. As a

teenager–in my Eastern religious phase–I thought it was sort of Zen-like. My Dad repeated the phrase several times in my life. Perhaps it was a phrase he heard from his Father, I don't know. It was a phrase I always remembered but never quite truly fathomed. Why it should cross my mind now was beyond me. Perhaps with that phrase, he was touching me so many years after his death. I miss him. I wish he could see this beautiful day.

I stretch my legs as I point my toes. It helps me nestle just a tad more comfortably in the lounger. Several women walk across my field of vision and, oh, so delicately, submerge themselves in the pool, which lies between the ocean and me. Two of the women sit at the pool edge. Slowly, the women in the pool come to the shallow end near them. They all begin the quiet chatter and laughing of friends having a very good time. I survey to the left of the pool and see a semicircle of empty chairs. They'll fill in soon, I think. With such great weather, everyone will be out today.

Behind my most-tinted sunglasses, I doze. The sound of chairs scraping concrete wakes me. Two women sit in the semicircle. The pool women are still there. Only the laughing and splashing, laughing and casting longing looks, laughing and kissing amongst them has increased. The day seems to have brought out the best in everyone.

Now, I'm no snoop or busybody, but I will tell you, the conversation of the two women to my left catches my attention. I like to hear accents. One of the women has that New York dialect that sticks way out in the South. Maybe that's the reason I take notice of the events that follow.

They speak of things as if they are new friends . . .

or new friends who want to be new lovers. It's good to realize that this early spring day might hold new beginnings for them. We all need the hope of a new beginning.

As the accented woman speaks about her last affair in New York, a van pulls up near the pool area behind them. Two women, engaged in a seemingly important conversation, emerge from the van. The driver, after a loud thunk of the door, heads for the semicircle without offering the passenger assistance. The passenger opens the side van door and begins to pull a striped fin–no, after a few more tries, make that a multicolored fish tail–from the van. I must say, I was charmed by the spectacle. Woman-watching is my favorite sport. I feel the scene unfold only for me. Everyone else has their backs to the van or are much too busy in the pool to notice.

With no success of removing the fish tail from its position, the woman leans into the van, and, hugging the middle of the fish tail creature, she pulls it from the confines of a back seat stuffed with blankets, beach chairs, and a couple of cardboard boxes.

That's when I get my first real look at the fish woman. The passenger is grasping the fish in front of herself with both arms and walking toward the pool. That is no ordinary inflated pool toy, my friend, but a *huge* multicolored fish that shimmers as the sun bounces off its metallic stripes. What the hugging of fish to woman creates is unique. Picture it. Walking toward you, a creature of, say, about 5'8", with flowing red hair that blows with abandon in the sea breeze. The humidity only adds to its unruliness. She has the smile of a vixen and flashing green eyes of Irish fables (I'll admit now, I only noticed her eyes later). It was one of those faces that

Renaissance artists loved to paint–beguiling, a little plump, but so sinfully sexual that you know you are going to hell for looking at it (Maybe that's why all those faces show up in religious art. It's a test). The smile of the fish woman is enough to make me want to find the nearest university course on mermaids and myths of the sea, right then and there.

From neck to ankle the lovely creature's true body is hidden from view by the height and breadth of fish. I just know she has the lovely ample breasts and hips also displayed in those Renaissance paintings . . . even her fish flesh is a marvel. It sheens and shimmers in the sun and sensually ripples as her walking brings her closer to the pool. The most precious and perfect flesh for a woman who could pose on a half-shell.

Her feet are bare. The sand slightly covers her toes as she walks. Those are feet more accustomed to walking the low water mark by moonlight, than being bound by shoes.

This blending of female appearance and oceanic form is just too delicious. As she sits in the semicircle by the pool, she kisses her fish on the forehead and carefully tosses her aquatic half into the pool. The lady who sits and dons sunglasses is just as striking as I imagined. The driver introduces her to the other two women and casual conversation ensues.

With enough material for a very pleasant dream, I nap. I awake to the fish woman gliding in front of me in the pool. Her fish body now buoys her as she travels from the middle of the pool toward the semicircle. Again, lovely arms hug the fish, as water flows down her bare back. Bare hips glisten with water splashes as her legs propel her poolside.

I am doubly blessed to see the front *and* back of

the beautiful creature. Other women, some bare, laugh and swim around her. They seem like mermaids playing with abandon in the ocean. There are eight or ten in the mythical sea, but only the fish woman, with wild red hair and sensual curves, catches the eye of the New York accent.

The fish woman emerges from the pool and her metallic skin. The accent offers a hand and a towel. Cozily and casually, the four-chair group talks by the pool. The fish woman sits, not by the driver, but by the accent.

I watch as the fish woman flashes green eyes and subtle smiles to the woman with the accent. Water trickles down her arms and breasts. The towel rests in her right hand, which lies on the chair arm. Her left hand runs through her hair and brushes back flyaway curls drying in the sun. A small patch of water nestles at her feet. Perhaps it is a tiny offering from the metallic striped fish.

The fish woman smiles, laughs, flirts, and seduces the accent. Who would not be charmed by the elegance of bare sensuality, lovingly kissed by water? The rhythm and purpose of the fish woman is slow, determined, and so very beautiful.

As their hands touch on the accent woman's chair arm, they agree to another meeting–a meeting no drivers or other new friends will attend.

It occurs to me, as I wipe the perspiration from my chest, that my Dad was right–"The fish will catch you."

THE END

Other titles from Creative Works Publishing

Captive Love by Koz St. Christopher. A college student finds herself aboard a luxurious cruise, on her way to a tropical island paradise. Kidnapped by a powerful businesswoman who longs for love, Rachel becomes a pawn in a game of seduction and power. Romance, erotica, martial arts, action and adventure.
ISBN: 1-930693-85-0   **200 pages**   **$13.95**

The Hope Chest by Victoria & Catherine McConaughy. A wonderfully depicted story spanning the years from The Great Depression to the end of WWII. *The Hope Chest* takes the reader on a journey through the victories and tribulations of a strong, yet gentle and caring lesbian couple, Marie and Abbey.
ISBN: 1-930693-90-7   **336 pages**   **$14.95**

Pursuit Of Passion by Victoria M. Brunk-St. Christopher. "Sex, love and rock-n-roll" is the theme of the 70's rock group, 'Purple Passion' and its lead singer, Jasmine Jacobs, who is pursued by a sexy, young groupie who rocks her boat making her want more, more, more!
ISBN: 1-930693-53-2   **248 pages**   **$13.95**

Love On Lesbos by Helena Lattimore. Set in Greece, a wealthy woman finds herself drawn into an international web of intrigue and terrorism by two mysterious, beautiful women who vie for her love. Romance, erotica, action and adventure.
ISBN: 1-930693-95-8   **196 pages**   **$13.95**

Stormy Desires by Victoria M. Brunk-St. Christopher. A love triangle involving two long-time lesbian lovers and a wealthy executive turns tragic for their families. Mystery, romance, erotica and adventure reveal the characters' stormy desires.

ISBN: 1-930693-54-0   216 pages $13.95

What Color Is Your Scarf? by Michael S. Brown. Life in the "Gay Lane" as experienced by a 40-something man discovering himself rather late in life. This "coming out" odyssey provides humor, insight and encouragement.
ISBN: 1-930693-93-1   108 pages $9.95

Lesbian Short Stories by Victoria M. Brunk-St. Christopher. Humor, romance, erotica, mystery and fantasy make up these eight lesbian short stories.
ISBN: 1-930693-81-8   112 pages $9.95

No Exceptions! A Gay Christian's Guide by Victoria & Koz St. Christopher. Written to encourage and reinforce the fact that there are NO EXCEPTIONS, according to Jesus, as to who can be a Christian. Based on John 3:16, this book is essential for anyone who has been told that you can't be gay *and* be a follower of Christ.
ISBN: 1-930693-55-9   80 pages $9.95

Playing In Traffic by Stan Purdum. Experience the romance and adventure of the open road as one bicyclist travels the full length of US Route 62 from Niagara Falls, NY to El Paso, TX. Filled with the author's humorous experiences, wry observations and fascinating encounters with the people who live along this byway which slices diagonally across America's heartland.
ISBN: 1-930693-86-9   236 pages $15.95

A Writer's Guide to Sassy Synonyms for 'Said' by Koz & Victoria St. Christopher. This wonderful thesaurus not only offers over 1,000 descriptive alternatives for "said" when writing, but also one or more definitions for each synonym, a sample

sentence demonstrating the proper use of each word and a quick reference guide. A MUST for writers.
ISBN: 1-930693-89-3   **168 pages**   **$14.95**

ABCs To Positive Living by Koz & Victoria St. Christopher. The positive affirmations in this book will help break the chains of destructive, negative thoughts and behaviors replacing them with the positive seeds necessary to cultivate a happier, more successful and fulfilling life in the future.
ISBN: 1-930693-84-2   **168 pages**   **$9.95**

No Need to Fear: Overcoming Panic Disorder by Victoria & Koz St. Christopher. The true story of one person who has lived with and overcome many of the fears associated with this disabling condition.
ISBN: 1-930693-87-7   **80 pages**   **$9.95**

Quit Smoking Using the Time Chart System by Victoria & Koz St. Christopher. Written for those who truly want to quit this book includes step-by-step instructions, incentives, charts, positive affirmations, relaxation techniques and more.
ISBN: 1-930693-88-5   **80 pages**   **$9.95**

The Elf Princess by Toria LaPorte & Julia Edwards. Discover the surprising fate of Lollia, a young, orphaned girl living at the North Pole and her parents, when they are magically reunited.
ISBN: 1-930693-94-X   **84 pages**   **$9.95**

IncrediBoy! Be Careful What You Wish by Lee Clevenger. An unathletic, unpopular boy is transformed into a superhero through the power of two rings, lost by an evil alien while visiting Earth.
ISBN: 1-930693-92-3   **200 pages**   **$11.95**